Pigswill and The Four Winds

Pigswill and The Four Winds

Michael Foot

Matador
9 Priory Business Park,
Wistow Road, Kibworth Beauchamp,
Leicestershire. LE8 0RX
Tel: 0116 279 2299
Email: books@troubador.co.uk
Web: www.troubador.co.uk/matador
Twitter: @matadorbooks

ISBN 978 1800462 496

British Library Cataloguing in Publication Data.
A catalogue record for this book is available from the British Library.

Printed and bound in Great Britain by 4edge Limited
Typeset in 11pt Aldine401 BT by Troubador Publishing Ltd, Leicester, UK

Matador is an imprint of Troubador Publishing Ltd

A big thank you to my daughter, Joanna Hawthorne, for the brilliant artwork for the cover.

Also a big thanks to my wife Michele and to Brendan & Joanna Hawthorne for reading both manuscripts with a measured eye and suggesting numerous improvements.

'PIGSWILL' is dedicated to all those around the world whose job it is to fight financial fraud in all ts forms. It's an often thankless task but it is and will always remain a vital one.

PIGSWILL

1

A quick CV on me to provide the background for this story. In short, I'm what would be called in 2019 (when I'm writing this), a white British stale male, reasonably well educated, who celebrated his 50th birthday in 2002. My marriage was no more by then, much to my regret now as I look back on things; and I saw very little of my children at that time. I've done better since with regard to my family, I'm glad to say. But there's no need to have my wife or children in this story, so that's just about the last you'll hear of them.

I do need to say a little about my early life, not least because of its heavy doses of old-fashioned Evangelism. One of my earliest memories – my childhood wasn't much fun and I've wiped most of it from the memory banks – was when I was about 4 1/2, just in primary school. Where I learned and then wrote out again and again the adage 'The Devil makes work for idle hands to do.' I learned lots more Old Testament by rote, not to mention most of Hymns Ancient and Modern. I must have been one of the youngest children in my generation to learn how the OT God loved to go round smiting his enemies and know only too well what 'smiting' meant. Thanks to 'Hymns Ancient and Modern' I also spent my early years thinking 'modern' must include the 19th Century. But it's amazing what you can get over.

Anyway, for whatever reason – and this endless religiosity is the obvious reason that comes to mind – I have always been virulently opposed to 'bending the rules' or breaching the morality code that I grew up with. I can well recall a couple of small vignettes to illustrate just how that affected me, from my earliest working life. Aged 17, I got a brief holiday job washing dishes for the caterers at the Wimbledon tennis fortnight. These were the days long before young people with ambition thought of things like 'relevant internships'. Rather, the Summer Vac was a time to earn a bit of money to try and keep the beer flowing through the thirsty days of Term. And 13 hours a day for 12 days out of 13 didn't seem a bad way of earning money even if it did involve – in a world before dishwashers – endless hand-washing of plates of strawberry and cream. But that 2 weeks – repeated the following year – was the first time I remember having my eyes opened to the array of subtle fraudulent practices that I now know goes on almost everywhere almost all the time.

For example, the daily newsellers all in those innocent days got given 1 or 2 general entry tickets for the early days of the competition. Newseller A, standing outside the ground, would sell his ticket to a member of the public and tell him to hand the ticket in to his mate selling the same papers inside the ground, as in those days – having gained access – he would no longer need the ticket. Seller B inside would receive the ticket and then, a few minutes later, wander out to stock up A's supply of papers to sell. The ticket would be returned to A and the process repeated.

There were lots of other little 'practices' that affected me more directly. It turned out that all the Managers of the various little restaurants inside the ground had a 'wastage allocation' designed to allow for natural wastage, for example because of fresh food going stale. (A 3-day-old bath bun is not a pretty sight nor – and I have eaten quite a few – is it particularly good to eat.) It followed in this strange little sub-world that, if a Manager could successfully pass off old stuff as edible or drinkable, they had an allowance, which they could use to take beer or cigarettes to an equivalent value, no doubt for onward resale. Stock control, where for example, your computer could give you an exact number at any time for the packets of fags on your shelf was, of course, still decades away. Though, of course – and I won't bother to elaborate as it takes us away from the timeline of the story – there are now plenty of ways of fixing stock control numbers if you want.

I very quickly learned through this regime that it was a major sin if I allowed the tea-urn to be still half-full after

5.30 pm. This was because of the 'allowance for wastage'. It was assumed that, at the end of the day, there would be some tea left over in the urn that would have to be thrown away – hence there was an allowance for wastage. But, in our case, at the end of the day, we were told to aim for an empty urn. If there was any remaining tea, it was syphoned off into jugs, which were then added back to each new urn brewed the next day. Thus there would be no wastage and more scope for the Manager to remove something of value. But syphoning tea wasn't much fun nor was pouring it back in unobserved the next day; so it became a game (it was a boring job) to have the tea urn run down to nearly nothing by the end of the day.

I can also remember that this was my introduction to small scale corporate bribery. These were the days before dishwashers – hence the need to pay students like me 5 shillings and 3 pence an hour (4 shillings an hour for the girls but they got tips so in the world of the 1960s that seemed fair enough to both sexes). One morning a management underling came in where I was working surrounded by plates that have been used for strawberries and cream. He pointed to one large pile and said *"Double-wash those"*. As a good employee, I did what I was told. About 20 minutes later he returned with a Council Health Officer; and you can guess which pile of washed-up dishes the Official took swabs from.

Thus does the simple soul learn – though at least I did come to realise that most of the people indulging in these practices were appallingly badly paid and clearly couldn't make ends meet the honest way. That helped me a bit. Likewise, the management demonstrated only too well in the second week that they didn't really deserve much better. We were lined up and told about the possibility of our working at the next event on their corporate agenda, which were the Buckingham Palace tea parties. As the management were only too keen to stress, it would be an incredible honour for us to be allowed to work there. To reflect that honour, our pay would be cut to 4 shillings an hour for everyone and of course there would be no tips. Lovely people the management. But, at least, the company organising all this teetered from disaster to disaster in subsequent years and finally disappeared, after displaying financial incompetence on a huge scale, into the maw of one of the giant conglomerates that grew up in the 80s.

I suppose, if I had to summarise, I'd say that it didn't take me long as a young adult to realise that, while I may have been taught that *'The mills of God grind exceeding slow, they grind exceeding small'*, an awful lot of people dropped off this mortal coil still clutching the proceeds of their greed. As far as I could see, the 'wages of sin' were not actually death but were often pretty healthy; I have to say that a lifetime's work trying to fight some of these practices hasn't changed my mind about that!

The other feature of my character, which again I seem to have been born with, was a strong desire to 'understand' everything that was going on around me. This is relevant now only to say that the desire for 'understanding' how something works and, thus, the desire to understand why people are so greedily stupid, have popped up and come together over and again in my life.

2

Early in spring day
Rising, you ask why it is?
Answer may kill hope.

Sorry. I realise I now need a short digression to explain that little poem, as I'm sure a number of them will appear before the end of this story.

It is an example of my version of a Japanese form of poetry called the HAIKU. The classical form of haiku has 17 'on', a word which I and many Westerners equate with 'syllable', though it really isn't. The verse is meant to come in 3 lines, respectively of 5, 7 and 5 'on'. It also traditionally has 2 other 'qualities'. The first is that 2 images or ideas are juxtaposed. In this case, 'early in spring day' and 'rising' juxtapose the ideas of

(a) being young and (b) getting up. And there needs to be a cutting word, a kind of verbal punctuation mark which signals the point of separation and which shows how the images are related. I use the word 'kill' for that. The second quality the haiku is supposed to have is a seasonal reference – I of course use 'spring' in the example above. As that particular haiku relates back to my learning experiences at Wimbledon in the late 60s, 'spring' is poetic license; it was really late June.

Thus, the poem actually refers to the idea that when you are young you rise in hope, as you also ought to do each day. But it goes on (sorry for the British pun) to say that experience may kill your optimism when your questions about 'why' get answered. If you think this is all a bit mad, I would just point out that the same idea was set out by Shakespeare, over 400 years ago in *Henry IV Part 2.*

The happiest youth – viewing his progress through,
What perils past, what crosses to ensue -
Would shut the book and sit him down and die.

I must have been 15 when I came across that Shakespeare. I was probably 60 when I remembered it and made it the basis for a haiku. Such strange minds we humans have that can summon early influences and have them reappear in different form decades later.

Anyway, after that poetic digression, back to my early life. Following my early holiday jobs, I enjoyed a pleasant but rather non-descript university life and, from there, found my way by stages to a City bank.

There I spent 20 years learning how to fit in, how not get on the wrong side of the grandees who tended to run each and every department; and, most importantly, how to help their messes go away when things went wrong. That was something they weren't terribly good at doing themselves and they tended to pay well to have their own and totally discreet Mr. Fixit at hand if need be.

So, during those years, I became exactly that, a Mr. Fixit – and it didn't take much, now as I think back. When things went badly wrong – and not necessarily in my own department which handled the tens of thousands of payments world-wide that we made each day in the bank – I would be asked to help with finding a solution. Sometimes, that would be as part of a team – with or without outside experts (with, if things were bad enough). Other times, it was alone. But nearly always the end-game involved getting rid of at least one or two middle management who had done something wrong or had failed to notice that the systems they were using were flawed. And, almost always, it involved helping rewrite process manuals, often using the problems identified to force the local management to use IT better and get somewhere further into the 20th Century. I should stress that it wasn't always wrong-doing or greed that had caused the problems in the first place. But, nevertheless, that did often feature.

Those of you who have experienced enough practical examples of human nature in the workplace will readily understand that such a role as Mr. Fixit is not one that endears you to those around you. Once your reputation is known, if you suddenly appear in a new Department, you might as well carry a flag saying *"something wrong here; investigation under way"*. And, usually, remedying that 'something' requires making yourself unpopular. You ask endless questions; and you always give the impression, however hard you try to empathise, that you're there in some kind of bad news role that will eventually blow back on the original inhabitants. They must have done something wrong for this mess to occur. You are there to sort it out. Usually they *have* done something wrong. And, yes, your reputation – probably your continued existence in the firm – rests on 'sorting it'.

I found at least some of these assignments interesting – thankfully. Which wasn't something I could readily say about my normal job. There, the main intellectual frisson was usually to be obtained by trying to work out which internal process would next be redesigned, automated and made unrecognisable. In such circumstances, little things that grate often stand out in the memory. I was – still am – a fan of the Scott Adams Dilbert cartoons, because the creator captures so well what it's like to be a small helpless cog in a large corporate machine, which is exactly what I felt at the time.

Just before that 50th birthday in 2005, I recall being sent a Dilbert cartoon that I had somehow missed when it came out. The 'joke' was that Dilbert was supposed to have a password to his IT systems that not only changed every 30 days but which would be 'difficult' – something that no-one trying to get into your system could work out that you might have used. No more wife's birthday; no more – one I do recall that led to a real-life fraud – memorable password phrases like 'gin and tonic'. To make it worse, Dilbert's new passwords had to have a minimum of 8 characters; they had to include at least one UPPER CASE letter, at least one lower case letter, at least one number and at least one piece of punctuation. Finally, as if that weren't enough, no 2 passwords could ever have the same character appear in the same place. Thus, if your first password started with an A, no future password could.

Sound crazy? Any idea how you remember what you eventually get the machine to accept, except by writing it down? Which kind of defeats the point. The galling part to me, though, and the reason why it sticks in my mind so is that my own bank had – about a month earlier – imposed an incredibly similar regime for its own passwords. My reality had caught up with the world of the cartoonist. For the first time, I really understood how Dilbert must feel. Perhaps it was time to do something about it.

Anyway, all this helps explain why that 50th birthday actually turned into something of a seminal event. By 2005, most large firms –certainly the bank I worked for – had worked out that older workers cost more (especially for pension rights) than younger ones (who typically missed out on things like pension rights). The longer-standing workers were also generally less easy to kick around in the endless restructurings that were so in vogue at that point (one thing – the penchant for restructuring – that hasn't changed since). I guess the 'old-timers' had come to expect certain standards from their employer about how they would be treated, which made them more tricky to mess with. And, perhaps most worrying of all from the point of view of the little god of Efficiency on whose altar anything could be sacrificed, the older the employee was the harder he or she would find it accept the new IT systems. Or the new IT-based compliance suites that had started by then to become the norm.

Anyway, about 2 months before that seminal birthday of mine, my employer offered a generous severance package to 'good leavers' over the age of 50. To explain to those who don't know the phrase, 'good leaver' basically means anyone who would agree to leave with reasonably good grace, half train their successor and not smash up their desk on leaving. I did the sums and decided this was for me. I was being offered cash to quit, plus a better and earlier pension than I could otherwise get. To which the Government would kindly contribute by allowing some of it to be taken tax-free up front. My employer was happy to offer early retirement; I had no family ties or responsibilities to keep me tied to the corporate wheel a day longer. And, slightly arrogantly – but it later proved an accurate assessment – I thought that my experience and skill set would probably buy me into quite a few contracts to do what I do best, short-term 'fixit' jobs around the City. It wouldn't be a case of retiring 100%, for good.

I knew from one or two of my older friends who had already tried something similar that consulting was a very possible avenue for future employment. From their experience, I realised that some of it might involve periods working in odd parts of the world – one of my contacts had ended up doing 6 months living in a yurt in Mongolia, working for the IMF or the World Bank. That didn't worry me – indeed, the prospect of a bit of sun and ex-pat life had always sounded quite good, as long as the yurt was luxurious. Although I'm not a great risk-taker, the whole package seemed to make sense; and I thought the likes of Mongolia could be avoided with a little care. I signed up and, with very little difficulty became a 'good leaving early retiree'.

Just 3 months after my birthday, I quit, handing over my desk to a young man of 30. He was as green as could be around the ears about the business of banking; but I thought he might – after he had learned a few lessons the hard way – turn out to be pretty good. For his part, he was pleased to see me go. It was a step up the ladder as far as he was concerned, though I knew – even if he didn't – just how many rungs he still had to go to get anywhere worth getting as, by then, most corporate ladders were being pulled down at least as fast as you could struggle up them. My boss was even more pleased to see me go, because another couple of similar departures would constitute the salary savings he had to make to get his next bonus. And, the morning after my retirement, as I recovered from quite a hang-over in a blessedly late care-free lie-in, I felt pretty good about things too.

3

Throw all up in air
Release from summer's round
Necessary purge.

That haiku reflects the decision to up sticks and launch out on my own. I'll leave you to decide what I was throwing up, other than the job.

I felt better still about three months later when I signed off on the long lease of a small apartment in a bloc on what was then the 'edge' between the City of London and the East End. In case you're ever in this rather fluid geographical kind of situation, I quickly realised that there is usually a good way to tell where the boundaries for each are round your property. In this case, quite literally, if I went out of my new door and walked

200 yards towards the City, a cooked breakfast cost £5.50; and most of the little eateries were anyway Pret a Manger or similar establishments, to whom 'cooking' meant heating up a pre-packed bacon roll. 200 yards to the right of the apartments, a proper cooked breakfast at a greasy spoon was £3.50 and there wasn't a Pret-style coffee shop in sight!

Since my marriage had collapsed, I had not owned a property. But, courtesy of my ex-employer and HMRC, there was now enough cash in my bank account for me to do something about that. I had decided very quickly that I wanted something close to the City, as most of my work friends were there and, if I was to get work as a contractor, I would need to stay 'available' to these people. House prices everywhere had been going steadily up for years and around the City probably worse than most, as people got used to mega bonuses. You could always tell bonus time just by watching the showroom of the one car dealer based in Canary Wharf – a place I for some years had to visit regularly for work. Ten months of the year, the showroom sported top of the market Range Rovers and the like. To be bought by bankers as part of their 'out of town weekend' luxury experiences. But for 2 months a year these were replaced or augmented by Porsches and Ferraris, the kind of luxury cars that you would only ever buy if money were totally unimportant to you AND if you wanted to 'make a statement' of just how well you were doing.

Anyway, I only needed a small place – but even so I knew it was going to take most of that tax-free 25% of my pension pot that the rules allowed me to take in cash on retirement. I also knew that there were only maybe 20 streets or little areas on the City edges which would be in the right general location, and not in the crazy price bracket and not looking like they were part of a third-world film set. (I've always enjoyed wandering round Brick Lane – living there has always struck me as something quite different.)

2005 was way before the growth of internet estate agents and so there were only about 5 estate agents who might expect to have property of the kind I wanted. Business was obviously brisk; several of the bigger chains had brand-new cars scattered parked around the office, the cars screaming the brand name at you in letters a foot high from their parking bay. I had started looking around as soon as I had decided to retire. But retirement itself kicked the action button. Within a week I had looked at the relatively limited number of options and made my choice. By the time you allowed for the searches and all the other modern paraphernalia of modern house-hunting, I was just into my third month of retirement when the papers were all there to sign. Just a month after that, I and my very limited set of worldly belongings (furniture – much of it new – and books mostly) were installed in what, for the first time for a long time, I could call home.

What had I bought? Well, one of the blocks that had caught my eye from the outset turned out to have 4 or 5 apartments for sale. Maybe I should have thought more about that at the time; but the smooth agent I dealt with was very plausible. The bloc had originally been the City HQ for a sizeable second-tier insurance company. In the mid-90s, the firm had decided to upgrade to the City proper; and the block had been converted to residential use just in time to catch the demand from Hong Kong nationals looking for bolt-holes abroad before China retook its old territory. The bloc had 109 flats in all of varying size, spread over 5 floors and with a few penthouse suites at the top (the penthouses quite out of my league or even thoughts). Over half the flats had originally been bought by Hong Kong nationals; and, after 5-6 years, these people had either activated their bolt hole or become more comfortable with their new regime. Those who were staying in Hong Kong were now selling down their holdings, taking advantage of a strong London housing market. That's what the agent said. Obvious really, certainly plausible.

I didn't make much fuss about the price – that's the kind of weak spot that appears when unusually there are funds in your bank account; but, frankly, I wouldn't have got the thing if I had made waves. I put my hand up now and admit that I certainly didn't think about what life (and London housing prices) would be like if the bottom fell out of the global financial markets as it did 18 months later. Who did then, let alone a bit later, say in late 2007, when the sky really was about to fall in? I also didn't worry much about what life would be like living there. I wanted to own not rent. The accommodation – 2 bedrooms in a smallish but comfortable ground floor flat – was what I wanted and where I wanted it. There was a long lease. Service charges didn't seem unusually high. The flat came with a numbered and marked parking bay, so the old Volvo I had clung onto over the years had somewhere to live too. I could afford the flat and I wanted to get on with the next stage of my life. Deal done.

Even before I had moved in, the first of my consulting jobs had been and gone; and, in many ways, it set the tone for the work that was to follow, so I'll explain what happened. And, if you think it's all a bit bizarre, welcome to the City.

You may never have heard of 'boiler rooms' though there was an excellent Ben Affleck film of that title that came out in 2000 that I would still recommend if you want to understand the phenomenon better. But, in essence, a boiler room is a high pressure selling point (hence the boiler) for shares of firms that have little or no intrinsic value. The managers of the boiler room usually create the companies themselves and give them just enough 'life' and plausibility to colour the shares and make them easier to sell onto impressionable mugs of whom there are, I now realise, an endless supply. (Think bitcoin 10 years later.)

What the companies supposedly did varied over the years depending on the investing rages of the day. (So, for example, in the mid-2010s no self-respecting boiler room failed to have a crypto currency firm on its books.) The shares would cost not too much, say £1 or so each. By the time one of the big firms found out about the new technology and bought into get control, the potential investor was assured by the boiler room salesman that the price would be £20 maybe £30 a share. Sadly, in reality, these firms did exist but they didn't actually do much and certainly were never going to come to the attention of the likes of Google or Apple who might have paid crazy prices. And, if the investor tired of waiting and wanted to sell their shares then, regrettably, when he rang the boiler room salesman, there was never a strong enough market to produce any buyers.

Most boiler room operations also had features that made some of their wares attractive to those who were seeking bolt holes for their money. For example, located in places where the authorities were never very active in monitoring what was going on in the companies listed with them; and where those authorities certainly never sought to tax income or capital gains. In those days – and probably still the case now but these things have a habit of moving on – an International Business Company (IBC) based in the British Virgin Islands was the vehicle of choice; but there were many other attractive locations. By the late Noughties, there were some 800,000 such IBCs in that one British dependency, BVI, alone – over half said to be owned by Chinese entrepreneurs.

For the boiler room, this was a great structure to go for. If an investor bought into a BVI company, then he was already more than half way to being able to 'forget' to declare to the British tax authorities the large profits he had been promised. The island had British law; if he bothered to check, the investor could see that a BVI IBC was a common, regular, vehicle. The island authorities would be happy to confirm that the company existed if the investor made the effort to check (few ever did). And a local lawyer or accountant would probably be listed as the point of contact for the company.

If, later, the investor got unhappy, he (nearly always a 'he') would get no help out of the local authorities on the island to 'have something done about it'. As far as they were concerned, everything was being done as it should. The contact point on the island for the company – if approached – would decline to say anything about the company *("our local law makes it a criminal offence for me to tell you anything of substance")*. While the UK authorities – if the investor was British and was prepared to admit to the UK tax man that he had invested a large amount of money in this way – neither knew nor cared about the company. And, in the unlikely event that the UK authorities agreed to ask the local government authorities, the chances of getting a meaningful answer (for example about the name of who really ran the company) were zero. The only thing the UK authorities did care about (or indeed could do much about) was if the boiler rooms were operating in the UK or perhaps in another EU country where some authorities took a dim view of such financial high jinks. So most boiler rooms were careful to operate just outside that net and it didn't take much to do it.

Anyway, this is a long intro into the case I ended up handling as my first fraud consultancy. One of the big accounting UK firms had been brought in by a group of aggrieved UK investors when it appeared that there was something horribly wrong with their investment. These individuals had between them put up about £15 million into a – wait for it – crocodile farm, Croc Rock.

The sales spiel had been aimed at the greediest and naivest of investors. They were promised a 'guaranteed' annual return of 50% – this at a time when any normal investment opportunity that offered more than around 5% a year was likely to carry substantial risks. The 'return' was to be earned by buying, breeding and rearing crocodiles who must have come from the same place that gave 19th century children the golden goose. The croc's skin was a high value product – obviously. The teeth – it was claimed – were worth a small fortune too, to the Chinese, no doubt offering some great boost to the male sex drive like several other products known to sell well round Beijing; and crocodile meat was both a delicacy and extremely low in cholesterol. There were great markets to exploit in the restaurant (and the boiler room) trade.

I got involved because one of my ex-colleagues recommended me when the audit firm brought in by the aggrieved investors asked its own workers to come up with some people who might be free immediately. The auditors had too much sense to think that an investigator would have any luck; but they were being paid and wanted a quick 'investigation and wrap up'. By the time I heard about it, things were already getting out of control. The croc farm – in Belgium! – was in the hands of the local version of the RSPCA there, once it had become apparent that the managers of the farm had fled and a lot of hungry crocodiles had been left who would quickly eat each other. The company bank account had been cleaned out; all the management people involved had disappeared.

In the event, it only took 10 days of my time to get to the bottom of the fraud (which was my remit) and only 3 of those days in Belgium. I also spent 4 largely fruitless days in Spain where the boiler room for the shares seemed to have been based. (In those days, the Spanish authorities weren't as fussy as they later became if their own nationals hadn't lost out and, of course, the number of British criminals safely located in the sun on the Costa del Crime have long provided a ready staff for any suitable local boiler room.) I suspect it took a lot longer for the Belgian RSPCA to rehouse their crocodiles than to determine the parameters of the fraud.

I'll give you the short and sweet version of what happened because, in so many ways, it encapsulates everything that's wrong with this greedy world and is the theme of this manuscript.

As I've already explained, investors were lured in by the offer of a ludicrously high 'guaranteed return'. Needless to say, on examination, the firm providing the guarantee had no assets and nothing from which the guarantee could be met. After that, the fraudsters did 3 beautifully simple things. First, there is no easy way any investor could work out what a real live crocodile would actually cost; that's not a price you'll find in the Financial Times. So, in the company books, the price of every croc bought was recorded as 4 times what the crocs actually cost. Second, the firm recorded 10 crocs bought for every one actually bought. So you have a solid basis for a 40 to 1 scam. Finally – and I thought this was a lovely touch – the firm claimed that Belgium was much more suitable for rearing crocs than England (exactly why was not explained). But every investor buying 500 shares was promised that one of the crocs would be allocated to them; and the crooks also promised that any investor was free to drop in to the farm in Belgium at any time, where 'their' croc would be available for them to see!

We never found a paper trail showing whether any of the investors took up the offer to see their investment. But, of course, if they had they would have been able to see plenty of crocodiles, one or more of which would have been presented as 'theirs'. Just maybe 50 crocodiles in all, not the 500 that the books suggested had been bought.

My task turned out to be relatively simple once I had understood the basis of the fraud. Shares were sold, crocodiles 'allocated' to investors and the money allowed to build up until the market for gullible 'crocodile investors' seemed to have been sated. Once new money coming in was down to a trickle, the company managers involved had cleared the bank account out and disappeared – where to I don't think was ever established. Leaving a couple of hapless Walloon cleaners and animal keepers to come in next day to find nothing left except hungry crocodiles. And of course a lot of investors who thus learned a lesson about greed the hard way. Or, rather, about the costs of being 'PIG-headed':

- **Prejudiced** (for example thinking that avoiding UK tax was innately a good idea),
- **Ignorant** (about the worth of a crocodile or the value of some guarantees),
- **Greedy** (that irresistible 'guaranteed 50 % a year return'.)

4

It's time now I introduced Mr U (or Mr. NON-U as he became later to some of us), because it was about now that I became aware properly of what I had let myself in when buying my lease. A note had been pushed through my door several weeks previously to 'remind' me that the leaseholders' AGM was due. Its location (a pub just down the road), date and time were given; but – which seemed a little odd given my very limited knowledge of such things – there were no documents (like an agenda, accounts or any of the things you might have expected).

When I checked at the Porter's Desk (more on that vital part of the infrastructure in good time), I was told that there was nothing more. And so, on the Wednesday evening concerned, as I had a free evening,

I set off on the 5 minute walk up the road to the pub where the AGM was to be held. I didn't get further than the Porters' Desk as a small tidal wave (more a sizeable dribble) of people came in just as I was about to leave. One of them saw me and, though I don't think he had any idea who I was, said *"No point in going to the AGM if that's where you're off to. That bloody man has got it called off; and we're all coming back to try and have a quick meeting here."* At this point, one of the others in the dribble joined in. *"Yes, apparently Mr Uranishi managed to frighten off the landlord of the pub, so that when we turned up he wouldn't let us use the room we'd booked; said there could be trouble and he didn't want any part of it."*

The next few minutes were disorganised to put it politely. The dribble continued until there were 25 or so people milling about. And at that point, one rather worn individual – who turned out later to be the Chairman of the Leaseholders' Committee – raised his voice and told everyone to head to the main entrance to the apartment carpark. Apparently, there would be enough room there for everyone to get together (although standing) and it might be possible to see if something could be saved from the wreckage.

I followed the new flow of people, having only a rough idea of where they were planning to go and, as we walked through the necessary corridors, I tried to tap a couple of my new colleagues as to what was happening. From them, the following 'facts' – though, of course, I had no measure of whether they really were facts – emerged:

1. Mr. Uranishi was a leaseholder who, with one other out of the 109 altogether, had been fighting a campaign for several years against the Leaseholders' Management Committee;
2. this fight had basically been by way of cases taken by Mr U to the Leaseholders' Tribunal alleging that money was being misspent by the Committee and should be reimbursed to leaseholders;
3. he had lost each case but only after the Committee had spent thousands of pounds on legal advice – which the leaseholders as a group had had to fund;
4. that fact, or another related, had typically led to another case going back to the Tribunal within weeks;
5. leaseholders – my 2 new colleagues asserted – had 'had it up to here' with the whole process, which was becoming quite widely known about and making it difficult for any leaseholder to sell on the open market (except to 'ignorant' people like me);
6. tonight's AGM had supposedly been, in part, to allow for another discussion as to how to stop Mr U;
7. but Mr U had persuaded the pub landlord that it would be in his interest not to allow his pub to be the site of what Mr U described as an 'illegal gathering'.

Who exactly Mr. U was seemed unclear. One leaseholder thought he was Russian, certainly Slavic, another that he was Oriental, possibly Thai. I later heard several other arguments as to his background. The man himself then turned up, accompanied by a rather attractive girl and a harassed looking TV camera man. The girl made sure the camera was running and then engaged a couple of the leaseholders in conversation, basically asking them if they weren't fed up with their money being wasted in fighting 'poor Mr. U'.

The leaseholders didn't feel that at all; and, as soon as it became evident what was happening, several other like-minded leaseholders gathered round the camera to add their pennyworth. Over the next 10 minutes the atmosphere became increasingly heated, with Mr U joining in the TV altercation, more leaseholders arriving and no sign of any calming or organising influence. I am not a great one for such contre-temps and decided to head back to my own flat, realising that any form of AGM was unlikely to be either possible or productive. Just as I headed off, the camera man, girl and Mr U disappeared down the flight of stairs to the carpark – in the middle of an ungainly melee of leaseholders wanting to state their own opinions pretty forcefully. I was told later that the police arrived about 20 minutes later to clear up the 'remains' but heard no more than that.

I can't say I lost much sleep over the incident or even gave it much thought in the next few days. It seemed pretty tangential to my 'new life' and my desire to get started on my new role as a consultant. A circular did turn up at the flat a week or so later, to say that the AGM was being rescheduled. And there were more updates over the following months, including news of another impending Leaseholder Tribunal case. But, by then, some of the first signs of what later became the Great Financial Collapse of 2008 were becoming apparent, if you chose to look in the right places. But work was piling up everywhere and most people were raking in better money than ever and extrapolating the good times forward for ever and a day. (Just go back and look at Gordon Brown's speeches as Chancellor at the time if you don't recall what it was like.)

For me, the next 3 years were something of a blur. Over the first few months, I got to know a few of the leaseholders, mostly over a drink. Several of them were on the Management Committee; and it was clear from what they said that this body was exhausted and quite out of its depth. A classic case, I thought, of a bunch of decent middle-class people unable to comprehend, let alone combat, a ruthless and unscrupulous opponent. But things staggered on, as they tend to do; and Mr. U kept on losing his Tribunal cases. As for me, I was having too much 'fun' or at least too much work to think very deeply about anything. And the work came rolling in for me too.

The next 'big event' I recall for the bloc was the 'mass directors' resignation, which must have around the middle of 2008. One morning, a letter arrived for every flat, stating that all the directors of the Management Committee had resigned; and, in the light of this, another company would take over the running of the building, the directors of which included Mr. U and his leasehold supporter. The following morning, another letter was pushed through every door in the bloc from the Management Committee, saying that the Directors had not resigned. Someone had written to Companies House with what must have been forged documents purporting to show that the Directors had resigned; and this new company, which had just happened to be waiting in the wings, had stepped forward to claim management rights.

At almost exactly the same time, the winds of what became the Great Financial Collapse of 2008-10 started to blow in earnest. Northern Rock had collapsed some time before; and for those of a nervous mind set, it was time to start thinking some 'what if' thoughts as other pillars of the financial edifice began to totter. I can even recall wondering what life under a yurt might be like if that's what it came to.

As it happened, I was off to Dublin the morning of that second letter. By the time I got back a couple of weeks later, a degree of normality had been restored. But the existing Committee had tried and failed to get the Metropolitan Police interested in the supposed forged signatures. ("No money has actually been lost, Sir, has it? How would we possibly track down who might have done it?") And this, for some of the Committee, was the last straw.

Unfortunately in catching up with all this in a late night drink with the MC people I knew, I made the mistake of saying I would stand for the next Committee. I suppose I felt sorry for a group I had got to know moderately well and who seemed to have run out of steam. And, rather arrogantly, I suppose I just thought of this whole lamentable issue as the kind of thing I fixed for a living. The Dublin trip had left me on a high – I was now locked into what promised to be an interesting project for months, looking into how some of the Irish banks – one in particular – seemed to have managed to lose all their capital and more in a mad conveyer belt of bad lending. Problems like Mr. U seemed tiny to me by comparison. 'My bad' as modern English would have it.

5

My forays to Dublin in fact lasted for many months, in fact, as the scene that unravelled there rapidly took on worse and worse colours. Virtually every local bank was bust and dependent upon an ever open tap of public (taxpayers') money to keep going. The forays were fun and not just because the Irish themselves are fun. I had never seen at close hand a banking cock-up of these proportions. And, once it became obvious that the damage had already been done, here was I being paid to conduct what was essentially a forensic post-mortem on how one bank had got into that state.

There were so many surreal elements to the situation I found that I'm spoilt for choice in even giving you a flavour. For example, I used to fly from City Airport (one of the benefits of my choice of apartment) to Dublin on a Monday morning and take a taxi into the main bank I was investigating. Dublin taxi drivers are as chatty as any I have come across. And, as soon as I'd specified the bank to visit, out it would all come, stories of bank stupidity, cupidity and ruthlessness as seen through the eyes of a small, closely-knit, community. There are two ways from the airport into Dublin. One is quicker – especially in the rush hour – and involves a tunnel for which you have to pay a toll. The other meanders. And I quickly found that, unless I specifically asked for the tunnel, the taxi driver would go the other way, just – as far as I could see – to prolong the time he had to tell me about the perfidies of the banking system rather than to make a bit more money. (When I thought about it, I could see they had a point. By this time the Irish government had poured huge amounts of taxpayer money into propping up the banking system; employment had collapsed, as had the housing market across Ireland. Everyone could plausibly argue that they were sharing the pain.)

When I got to the bank, there was always an Alice-in-Wonderland air about the whole place. Most of the senior management had gone when the bank had been nationalised. But those who were left had generally taken a very active part in creating and implementing the disastrous lending policies that had brought the bank to its knees in the first place; and, in most cases, as the senior people had come under fire and been forced out, many of the next rung had actually found themselves promoted. This wasn't a case of the innocents now being left in charge. And the only thing those left behind seemed genuinely upset about in all this was not their own part in bringing the bank down but that the Government had taken away their free tickets to the Irish rugby internationals at Lansdown Park.

Indeed, a few weeks after my arrival, the bank management decided staff morale needed to be boosted. They couldn't expect to clear up a 'bad bank' if they weren't happy; and the fact they were still in work wasn't enough. Their solution? The reintroduction of a coffee break of 20 minutes in the morning complete with free pastries and sausage rolls. I never told that to any of my taxi drivers; but it seemed wonderfully apposite. The wages of incompetence, if not sin, in Ireland clearly stretch to sausage rolls.

My nights were spent in the local 5 star hotel. The first time I checked in, the Receptionist asked, with a fleeting smile *"Would you like to check in or buy the hotel?"* Almost every business was bust it turned out, and the hotel was no exception. After about 2 weeks, I caught on. There were no For Sale signs anywhere and I hadn't initially noticed. Everything was for sale but there were no buyers.

The actual work in the bank itself was hugely interesting. I had all the loan documents, the Minutes of the bank Loan Approval Committees, the freedom and the time to wander through them and talk – at least to the bank participants. I had started with the clear expectation that there must have been financial skulduggery to bring this bank down – most probably backhanders from potential borrowers to bank staff who could get their loans approved. To cut a long story short, months later when I had finished, I had a very different picture. Basically, an insanely optimistic set of lending policies driven by a management for whom growth was the only yardstick and combined with wholly inadequate checks at the outset. Worse, once the loans had started running, nothing like enough attention had been paid as to how the loans were actually proceeding. Plus (as if that weren't enough) no serious work to take and secure any collateral for the loan that might be available – at least until the loan had hit the rocks, by which time it was too late.

And – just one last moan – an almost complete absence of basic procedures – like checking on the linkages between borrowers. At one point, I discovered that 'my bank' had ended up owning in default about 70% of the building land available in large parts of Dublin – purely because they had had an attractive and heavily marketed scheme to finance new house building and had made no effort to put all that lending into a bigger picture. Corruption I couldn't find anywhere, which I later reckoned had to be good news. To put it in terms I shall come back to repeatedly in this book, these losses were primarily the result of ignorance and greed (for bonuses, for the kudos of growing faster than the rival bank down the road), combined in this case with a high degree of professional sloth which, if you like, you could define as prejudice against the need to worry about boring things like taking collateral.

In between my visits to Wonderland, while back in London, I picked up some more of the threads of the stories around Mr. U. And a mixed bag they were. In his favour, one had to admit that the running of the apartment bloc had left something to be desired, though the Committee could fairly point out that they were left no time by Mr U's constant attacks to do anything more productive.

It was also painfully obvious that the legal advice the Committee had been getting was at best slow, naïve and reactive – plus unbelievably expensive. Now I have to aim off a bit here because I never have liked lawyers; but this City firm of solicitors took the biscuit no matter how you looked at it. They had had no strategy and had provided the Management Committee with no leadership, just invoices. It seemed obvious to me that the Committee was never going to take on Mr. U successfully unless it developed a proactive policy, and hit back where it would hurt him. That was as far as my thinking had got. But, on the rare occasions where I thought about the problem in abstract, the first two steps seemed obvious – find a new Managing Agency to run the daily affairs of the bloc and find a new, aggressive, lawyer.

Little by little, I also came to discover that what was going on in our bloc was being replicated in many other completely unconnected cases, though never it seemed with the personal animosity that had developed in our case. The best explanation I got of this was that the new Labour Government in the late 90s had brought in changes to leaseholder law designed to protect leaseholders better. But these changes had been abused by aggressive leaseholders looking for trouble; and the changes to the law had made that possible by making it easier and cheaper to attack management committees in what was known then as the Leaseholders' Tribunal (LT).

Sometimes it was obvious what the attackers wanted – which was to get the bloc under their own management. That, depending on the circumstances, could lead to the very dubious – like getting control over the awarding of contracts for the management of activity (security, porterage, cleaning and so on); or it could lead to much more understandable things, like the leaseholders buying out the freeholds or paying for significant upgrades to services (with increased charges to match). What Mr U was after we never found out for sure though we eventually suspected the worst when, at several LT Hearings he appeared represented by a lawyer with close connections to a couple of very dodgy property companies. But, maybe it was mainly/all personal – who knows? However, I mustn't get ahead of myself.

6

The next AGM took place about a year later and this was where I joined the Management Committee. Mercifully it passed without incident, not least because someone on the Management Committee had had the sense to book it into a nearby university building which had the merit of also having its own security. Neither Mr U or his main supporter showed up and only about 35 leaseholders – all fed up with the endless expense but generally supportive of having no truck with Mr U. I was duly elected to the Committee (that was September). By Christmas, Mr U had given notice of another LT Hearing being brought and the Chairman of the Committee had resigned, saying he could take no more. Muggins at this stage made his second mistake and said he would take on the Chair; I could see I at least had more time than many of the mostly younger professionals who made up the leaseholders; and I also had my 'plan' for how to get us out of the hole. Finally, I still felt sure Mr U was in the wrong and that 'right' needed to be done. Naïve? Yes. Arrogant? Probably. Personally stupid? Undoubtedly.

Looking back, I can see now that I was indeed terribly naïve. Some parts of my plan were easy enough to implement. It turned out, for example, that there were a number of management agencies who could run the building day to day; and we reasonably quickly chose one who seemed both competent and not too fazed by the threat of Mr U. What I hadn't allowed for though, was that the existing agent was in semi-collapse and that much of the transition from old to new was complex, paper-heavy and just plain difficult. About 20 of the leaseholders had sub-let their apartments and many of these owners were in Hong Kong; these were unused to responding even to the simplest of requests, such as amending direct debits and standing orders to reflect the change of Managing Agent. It turned out too that the existing agents had allowed quite a few creditor accounts to go unpaid for a bit and pile up, so we were suddenly faced with demands for about 3 months of expenses in the last month of the year, as these situations were put right prior to the handover.

Finally, over time, I also came to see at first hand what I now think actually is endemic in British support services. And that is that, behind the relatively plausible and presentable people that a support firm uses to face out to its clients, the people who actually do the work behind the scenes are not very literate and basically don't care much. Shades of my Wimbledon management of over 25 years earlier. So bad was the level of literacy at the Managing Agent I ended up requiring prior sight of all communications being sent by the agents to the leaseholders, rather than have to live down, after the event, phrases *'this effects you'* or some such nonsense appearing on every letter the agent sent out. (Of course, since then this problem has become an epidemic and now I just grunt and move on; but it was less common in those days and certainly not what the leaseholders would expect from a Management Committee comprised supposedly of City professionals.

The search for a new lawyer was more tricky, not least because – how shall I put it – our existing law firm was quite clearly going to take us for every penny of fees it could before we moved; and they were clearly going to be bloody-minded about things like handing over files to the new lawyer in good order. (Their first suggestion I recall was that we should pay them to put their files into shape.) It was only some limited comfort, later, that the firm disintegrated a few months later. We had 4 presentations from would-be new lawyers to us. Fortunately, only one of them provided what we all on the Management Committee agreed we needed, which was a strategy to deal with Mr U. If I remember correctly, the same 5 members of the Committee came to each presentation and the decision at the end was unanimous. Certainly no need for me to enter the fray. And our choice eventually turned out a winner I'm happy to say.

Less pleasantly, I also rapidly discovered that the politics inside a bloc like ours was often white-hot and usually because people – even seemingly mild-mannered professionals – were always trying to get something for nothing. An early case I can recall involved a leaseholder who claimed that one of the porters had made him wait 15 minutes to deal with some simple issue, as a result of which the man had missed his flight from City Airport. He now wanted the Management Committee to reimburse him for the £250 extra cost he said he had incurred. Long letter, meeting with the aggrieved, a special hearing for him with the MC on which he insisted; all to produce the inevitable result – us saying he needed to manage his own time better, him swearing undying dislike of the Management Committee.

And then there were the other issues, like the tramp who had been allowed by one of the porters to set up home on a disused corridor and took some considerable encouragement to move on; or the spat – which I never get to the bottom of – of whether the leaseholder of Flat 30 was a 'lady of the night' or just rather free with her late-night invitations! It turned out that this was all part of the job of running the MC but not one that I was fitted for.

Life nevertheless began to settle down into some kind of rhythm, despite the fact that my paid work was happily frequent and, when going on, was nearly always 110% full on. The porters, the Head Porter especially (who it turned out loathed Mr U and therefore could not be trusted or left to do anything involving him), unfortunately came to regard me as the go-to person for any kind of problem. I had thought of myself as a Mr. Fixit; this was just at an uncomfortably low level of fixing. The Head Porter developed the unnerving habit of waiting outside my door in the early morning if he knew I was in 'residence' or of leaving an **URGENT MESSAGE PLEASE CALL ME** on my door. Mr U also somehow got to know something of my movements; and certainly from the moment I became Chair of the Management Committee I could be sure that any job that took me out of the UK would always be accompanied by the unveiling of Mr U's latest complaint or sally into the Courts. In successive weeks I touched down on a Caribbean island (a money laundering investigation) and then in Gibraltar (a dodgy insurance investigation) only to switch my mobile on, to find urgent calls from the Managing Agent or the Head Porter, for help in dealing with Mr.U.

Perhaps the Head Porter's best 'stupidity' – and nothing whatsoever to do with Mr U – was the day I found him at 7.15 am outside my door, waiting to say that a brick had fallen off the building and been found by someone passing by. The Head Porter claimed he could see where the brick had come from though, when I tested that, the point on the building he identified was so high that it was a matter of conjecture as to what, if anything, might be missing. My eyesight was certainly not up to it. I was in the middle of a hurried investigation, though this was fortunately in the City, so I had little time to spare.

Over the next few hours I managed to keep the paid job going and:

a. telephone the local council (*Nothing we can do Sir, we suggest you have the relevant piece of pavement fenced off; and of course any damage that does occur to anyone will be down to those running the building);*
b. hired 2 abseillers – both South Africans who, for £250 a day each were willing to come that day and abseil down to check the area from which the brick was thought to have come;
c. late in the day – it was mercifully summer and the evenings were long – get back, go up to the roof and be shown what the abseillers had found.

Answer? Absolutely no sign of any missing brick or of any structural problem on the outside of the building. The main abseiller thought that the offending piece of masonry had not come from any part of the building but had probably fallen off a lorry that had gone round the sharp bend on the busy main road that ran outside the bloc of flats. (This was a peak time for construction work in and around the City and a very plausible explanation.) The Head Porter had made himself scarce. I was left to ponder the lessons of the day, which inevitably centred round finding a new Head Porter.

7

As I said earlier, the distinguishing feature of our new lawyer was that he had a strategy to get on more even terms with Mr U and his solitary known supporter among the leaseholders. Both by now owed substantial past services fees, which they had refused to pay on the grounds that these costs had been incurred unreasonably. Our new lawyer pointed out that – provided our 2 opponents had borrowed on mortgage to buy their leases (a reasonable assumption given what we knew about them) – then the mortgage companies, like us, would have very good reason to want to see these past fees cleared. Otherwise, as the leases fortunately made clear, neither Mr U nor his friend could sell their lease – nor could the mortgage company intervene in the event of a mortgage default – because the Freeholder would not allow the lease to be transferred if fees remained outstanding.

I checked on this last point by tracking down the freehold company to a non-descript part of South London. I rang ahead and eventually found it, a large grey office building where I discovered on my visit that they handled nearly half a million freeholds where leases had been sold on the properties. A company name you and I would never have heard of. And yet, if you assume at a very conservative minimum that they took in ground rent of £100 a property (we were certainly paying more than that), you had a firm taking in £50 million a year just from that line of business. Add in the fact that every time – for example – you bought or sold one of the leases you had to pay them whatever they deemed reasonable to put the change through to their records. And you are looking at a pretty nice line of business, with almost no visibility, and no risk from recession or from almost any other risk.

Here I had a real bit of luck because the middle-aged woman who came to collect me from the Reception Desk turned out to know of Mr U. He had turned up out of the blue some months earlier and, as this woman hadn't been around, he had met someone more junior. He had then made the mistake of trying to browbeat the girl into providing a list to him of all the outstanding leaseholders in the bloc. And, when he had failed in that endeavour, he had ended up shouting at the kid – having, in the end to be removed from the building by their Security. So, the woman was absolutely clear from the outset with me that Mr. U would get no help from them and confirmed that their rules in this case were quite clear. No lease could be transferred if service charges were still outstanding – and the freehold company would always check with the Management Company before signing off on a change of lease.

It was also the fact, our lawyer had established, that in an earlier case brought by Mr U's friend against our Management Company, the High Court had made a very helpful ruling on costs. Typically, our original solicitors hadn't fastened onto this and pressed for it to be carried out, for it was actually a great stick with which to beat Mr. U. The appellant had lost his first case in the Leasehold Tribunal against the unreasonableness of some of the bloc's expenses. And, no doubt encouraged by Mr. U, he had gone on to appeal that decision in the High Court where, again he had lost. This time, perhaps because even the High Court had sensed that the appellant was just using the Courts to play a game, the High Court ruled that Mr U's friend was liable for a large share of the Management Committee's costs of having had to face the Appeal which, in the Court's view, had been without merit.

Like the service charges, our solicitor confirmed, these costs would have to be settled before any sale of the lease could be completed. Our lawyer also thought the mortgage company would be very willing to put pressure to get these sums paid off so that, if need be, the mortgage company could take action quickly if the mortgagor defaulted on the mortgage. From our point of view, of course, any money paid either to reduce outstanding service charges or to meet past legal costs would go straight into our funds and help to reduce future bills. By the same reckoning, any positive result here would greatly help to calm the groundswell of unhappiness among the leaseholders who **were** meeting their obligations.

So, that is the action we started. Finding out who were the lenders to the 2 apartments concerned turned out to be reasonably easy; and our lawyer thought that the fact that they were both mainstream lenders would also prove helpful. After a silence of about 3 weeks, we found that – quite by chance – we had hit pay dirt. The lender on the flat belonging to Mr. U's supporter turned out to be very interested in what our claim actually consisted of – amount, source and legal background. From that, our lawyer deduced that the mortgage was probably already in arrears. And, as we were just entering the real financial downturn, Mr. U's friend could not do what would probably have been possible before that point – refinance the mortgage with another lender and increase the size of the loan at the same time. As Warren Buffett had said some little time before, we were at that point in the economic cycle where you could see who had been swimming without trunks on. We very much doubted our opponents had ever had any trunks.

Weeks dragged by (how slowly lawyers move). But eventually we arrived in a really good place. The mortgage lender was taking over the mortgage and selling the flat with vacant possession. And it agreed that we would have first claim on the resulting money, to meet the service charges due (about £12,000 by now if I remember correctly) AND, more importantly, the

£30,000 or so that the High Court had awarded in costs which was the share of this supporter. To put the icing on the cherry, the Freeholder had also confirmed in writing that it would not transfer the lease to any new owner until our lawyer had in turn confirmed that all our costs had been met.

I don't remember many periods while I lived at The House (which is what all the inhabitants called the bloc) when I felt particularly happy; but this period was one of them. I don't remember exactly how long it lasted (I don't keep a diary). But I do remember the day it ended! I had just got off a plane – having arrived at one of the smaller British Dependencies that periodically called in specialist advice from London. I was there to handle what turned out to be a simple fraud case (more on that in a minute) and I was looking forward to a few days of warm sun and relatively easy work.

That – i.e. when I had just left the country – was typically when Mr. U had made his next move. As my mobile text message explained when I arrived in the sun, Mr. U had done 2 things. He had complained to the Law Society about the professional ethics of our lawyer. More worryingly for me – I thought our lawyer more than capable of handling any attack on him – Mr. U had lodged another case in the Leasehold Tribunal. This one asserted that the Management Committee had spent some £800,000 in 'unreasonable expenses' which should be paid back to Mr. U and all the other 'innocent' leaseholders. The sum amounted to some 2 years of total service charges levied; and, although I, of course, had only been on the Management Committee for a few months and had been Chairman for even less time, it was pretty obvious who was going to have to organise the defence, find the money to pay for that defence. And – if we lost – that same person would have to find some way of reimbursing leaseholders for money that was long since spent and gone.

8

I felt a bit better after checking into the hotel (it was over 30C, the hotel was right on a lovely waterfront on the island) and talking to our lawyer back in London. One of his best features, for me, was that he seemed to love challenges of the kind Mr. U was now posing. You could almost hear the zest in his voice as he talked over the phone. Nevertheless, the incident was a poor start to the trip. Our lawyer thought that the defence bill might easily tot up to another £30,000 – i.e. roughly what we had had to pay during the initial High Court action. And this time, there was no prospect of getting any reimbursement even if we won on every count. The Leasehold Tribunal had agreed to hear the case. The rules for the Tribunal were clear; each side bore its own costs. And, our lawyer went on to warn, it wasn't often that the

Tribunal ruled wholly in favour of one side or the other. Once you went down into the detail of expenditure on something like The House, he implied you were always likely to find some items of spending that, with hindsight, wouldn't look too clever. He thought the best we could hope for would be a substantial win; but that we'd have to work out, ahead of the result, how we would reimburse any money that the Tribunal did decide had been spent unreasonably.

Fortunately, it's not easy to stay too fussed about anything when the weather is 30C and above, the sun is shining and the rum is plentiful. And I might as well tell you a bit about why I was out there – both because it will help you understand the pretty good life I was by now leading and because the 2 cases I ended up dealing with each illustrate an aspect of the general point I'm trying to make in producing this little story at all.

The first was a rather sad case, because of the individual concerned; but it was a kind of fraud that appeared a lot around the world between about 2009 and 2012. It even had its own name among the cognoscenti – Article 419 fraud, named after the Article in which the Central Bank of Nigeria tried to deal with it in domestic Nigerian legislation. And, although Nigeria was not the only place where this kind of fraud originated, it was certainly a central point for it.

Basically, there were 2 main types of this kind of fraud. The first would start with an email to some mug's home web address. These emails were usually appallingly typed and ungrammatical; but, as the aim was to imply to the reader that they were dealing with an 'innocent' local, the misspellings and so on were probably all part of the act. The text would say something like this: '*Hello, my name is Frank Ocupu and I am residant of Lagos Nigeria. I am owner of many US dollars – $326,020.66 – and I need YOUR HELP to get these dollars out of my country. You see, our FOREIGN EXCHANGE laws do not allow me to hold these dollars although they were legitimattely earned by work I have done for WORLD OIL COMPANY here in Nigeria. I am in recete of your name as a man who can act quickly and look after his own. ALL YOU HAVE TO DO is email me the details of your bank acount. I will transmit the money to you immediately. You contract to send me half back to my acount – I am allowed to keep $ that have come to me from abroad like from you. You can keep the rest for fasilitating me. Please reply most quickly and in utmost confidence I am your Humble Servant Frank Ocupu M.A.*'

I wouldn't be surprised if, between say 2009 and 2014, a thousand Brits and Heaven knows how many other nationals fell for this. What usually happened then – if you responded – was one of 2 things, depending how well the fraud was organized. The well organised ones just cleared out your bank account once you had kindly provided the details. The less well organized would email back and say something like '*So sorry. Local bank manager requires gift up front to undertake to move my money to you. Please send £1000 in cash via Great Western, for collection by me in person at Market Square Branch Lagos. If you do this before 9 a.m. in your day, all $326,020-66 will be with you by end of day. Please do not fail me, I am in great need your Humble Servant Frank Ocupu.*' The money you dispatched – if you were so foolish – would of course disappear and Mr. Frank Ocupu would never be heard of again.

Anyway, what I was in the Caribbean to deal with was the second common version, which was why someone (the local Central Bank in this case) was paying my costs. I was there to give evidence as an Expert Witness. Some poor sod – no doubt like the stupid Brit in my example above – in the case to be heard had been so dazzled by talk of huge sums stuck in Nigeria that he had appeared some months earlier at a major bank branch in the capital of the island where I now was. With a Bankers' Draft for $81 million, yes $81 million drawn on the Nigerian branch of a well-known international bank.

Now, a Banker's Draft is like a cheque which a bank holding the money concerned issues to the depositor, who can then cash it relatively easily at an independent bank. That bank pays up and gets the cash back from the bank that issued the Draft, through SWIFT or one of the other international money exchange arrangements that the banks have between themselves. Our man had (I presume he had bought them at the same time as the Banker's Draft) a complete set of beautiful and colourful engraved certificates to give colour for his story. These 'showed' how the holder had 'earned' the money over about 5 years, providing oil exploration and other services in Nigeria to an international oil company. Five certificates in all, detailing the original contract, the invoice for the final amount, the acknowledgement of the debt by the oil company, the transfer of funds to the Nigerian bank and, finally, Central Bank of Nigeria's giving approval to the money being transferred abroad. Works of art, each and every one.

Of course, what had happened was that, as soon as the man had presented himself and the Draft at the local bank on the Caribbean island, the local police had been called. And, as far as I could tell, the poor man had spent the whole intervening period in the town jail (which could not have been a picnic), presumably because they were afraid he would do a runner, off the island, if released. The police had never managed to get him to shift his story and so they had never established that he (or how much he) had paid for the false documents. He was elderly – and, when I saw him going into Court – looked seriously down on his luck. How desperate do you have to be to risk possibly a lengthy jail sentence on a Caribbean island and part with whatever money you do have for a handful of what to any sane person have to be forgeries? He looked that desperate.

Anyway, the point of this short story is that often – if I'm right about what happened in this case – it's not the big fraudster who ends up in the dock but some little guy who is seduced by big numbers and the prospect of easy money. How I wished that the author of these and no doubt huge numbers of other forgeries had been in the dock. That would only have been appropriate. But I was there just to do my job, which was to appear as a prosecution witness to attest to the implausibility of the defendant's whole story and to explain how Article 419 fraud works.

Small miracle, well actually 2 small miracles. First, the Court met on the morning it was supposed to – I guess the Government had made clear how much they were spending on my per diem expenses, so delay was probably out of the question. Though it would certainly have fitted with local custom, which was to spin cases out for as long as possible and then at the end, if possible appeal the outcome to the Privy Council in the UK. An even better (second) small miracle for me – I had no interest in the outcome of all this save a general desire to see some sort of justice done – was that the Judge had thrown out the case by lunch. When I appeared as the first prosecution witness, he made it very quickly clear that, despite my supposed (indeed my actual) expertise, nothing I was saying about this case resulted from knowledge of the specific case nor of whether any of the documents involved were in truth forgeries. *"All your evidence is hearsay, Mr Carter"* intoned the Judge. *"I can see from the documents presented by the Prosecution that they have nothing directly from the Central Bank of Nigeria that relates to this case. The Prosecution case is irretrievably damaged, if – as is the case – I cannot accept that your testimony is based on hard fact on the case in hand. I am therefore forced to rule that the case should be dismissed and the defendant should be allowed to leave the island forthwith."*

Sometimes you get a decent result, even if by roundabout means. Certainly, as I enjoyed a Sundowner at my hotel that evening, I concluded that sometimes things have an odd way of evening themselves out. This man had lost money, spent time in remand in an unpleasant local jail, and I guessed would never go near another 419 scam in his life. If anything, he had suffered considerably more than he had deserved; after all he had just been incredibly naïve and very greedy but probably also desperate. There but for the grace of God go how many of us. The real villains escaped scot free but all too often that seems to be life.

9

The Central Bank wasn't too happy about the Judge's ruling but there was nothing to be done. And Caribbean residents tend to have a marvellous way I've found of rolling with the punches and coming up smiling. The very next morning, before I'd even had time to find out when I could book my flight back to London, I was called at my hotel by a Central Bank official. After commiserating over the failure of the case, he eventually got to the point of his call. *"As you're here, we wondered if you could just help us on something else that's come up. The honest truth is that we have a few banks and securities firms here who deal for clients on US Stock Exchanges – often for foreigners. To be frank, our bank supervisors don't know much about securities; but we've had a demand from the US Securities & Exchange Commission to investigate a case of potential insider trading that has used a local firm.*

You probably know that we are geographically pretty dependent on the US; and in fact, to keep them happy, we signed something last year to say that our local laws on confidentiality wouldn't apply to cross-border transactions in US securities that originated here. I don't think we ever thought that would come to anything. But now they've sent us a whole pile of transactions done on the New York Stock Exchange – but initiated here on island. And the SEC are demanding that we investigate for them and, if appropriate, help them prosecute any insider trading. To make it worse, the deal we signed last year said we would respond to requests within 10 days. No-one here has any real idea what to do. We thought, given your background, you might be able to help. Shouldn't take more than a few days and, of course, we'll continue the per diem payments and the hotel."

From my point of view, this looked like a no-brainer. Insider trading I knew all about, though I stress I've never had any first-hand knowledge. And if the local regulators didn't know what they were doing, I should be able to get a few more days of sun, rum and local colour with ease. I agreed to go into the Central Bank after lunch, took a late relaxed breakfast and went swimming. It was mid-February; 82 degrees Fahrenheit or 30 degrees centigrade, with not a cloud in the sky. What's not to like?

Now, if you're not familiar with insider trading, this is actually one of the easier financial crimes to describe. In a country like the US it is – and has long been – a crime to use any inside knowledge about a company or, say, a change in Government policy to benefit yourself or others by buying or selling securities. Suppose, for example, your brother-in-law works for a firm and he tells you over a weekend drink that his company has just won a huge order that will double the size of the firm. Monday, before the company's got around to telling the world about its success, you go and buy loads of its shares. A day or so later, the company announces the new order and its shares rocket. You quietly sell out. You've successfully been an insider trader. For anyone at the SEC to prove that you have, if you had done this trade on a US stock exchange, they would need to find your share transaction (when there could be thousands of share transactions a day), AND prove that you had got hold of the information illegally. Now, your brother-in-law is hardly likely to spill the beans even if he ever hears about the accusation. You're safe. And, if you are in any doubt about your safety (or if you do this regularly because you know lots of people in business and they talk to you a lot) you can always put in a safety valve. Share the info and the profits with a couple of friends. Get one of them to buy and sell the shares when you hear the price-sensitive information and split the profits with them. They return the favour in due course when it's their turn to receive something interesting. Now, there's not even a clear link between your brother-in-law, the share transactions and you.

Another way of putting a gap between you and the transaction, making it harder for any regulator to track you down afterwards, is to use a foreign securities firm to do the trading for you. Towards the end of my time at my UK bank, it had been common knowledge, for example, that a ring of British insider traders had taken to using a Monaco-based firm to do its trading, knowing full well that no foreign regulator had ever had any help from the Monaco authorities to track down dodgy share dealing. Add in the complexities of modern business; for example, there can be up to 400 insiders in a major proposed take-over by the time you've added in the executives, the lawyers and accountants of both sides of the negotiations. If one of those decides to give his brother-in-law or father-in-law a quiet heads up phone call the day before the take-over is announced, whoever is going to track that down after the event? Even less likely if the relative uses a foreign intermediary to buy and sell the shares! I could readily see, in the current case I was being asked to look at, why anyone would think that a trade in New York initiated out of a firm in a nearby independent island would avoid most of the risk of an insider dealing investigation.

Once you hear all that, you might wonder why I was reasonably happy to take on this request from the local central bank. My thought process had been fairly simple, though, and much more positive than the above. This was a small island, so the facts and figures about any share trading that I might need should be close at hand and easily obtainable. Second, I knew the SEC had a fearsome reputation. So, my guess was that they would already have obtained the key facts in New York and had now passed them, gift-packaged to the central bank; what the SEC needed was to avoid the confidentiality provisions in local law through the use of this Agreement they had signed. If that was the case, it should be relatively easy for me to confirm the facts relating to the local traders' actions. And, if things didn't go well, the worst outcome for me would be a few days of paid work in a nice warm environment.

When I turned up at the Central Bank (I knew better than to get there before 2.30 p.m. – the earliest time a local would deem acceptable for a meeting after a leisurely lunch and a short siesta), my hopes proved well founded. The Swiss-owned bank that was thought to have conducted the share trades in New York on behalf of its client was only about 200 yards away from the Central Bank. Very easy on these islands to keep close to all the financial people who matter. And I had been right about the SEC's zeal in tracking down the information which they had needed to deduce that insider trading had probably occurred. Dates and copies of the documents generated by the buying and selling of the shares on New York Exchange, information about the local firm that had sent in the orders, even all the details of the trading account through which the deals had been booked – they were all there in black and white. All the local Central Bank man had had to do had been to walk the 200 yards to the bank, armed with a short legally-worded demand from his lawyer to obtain all background documents on the client and – seen from the island – the pattern of transactions. And – even better for the locals – it appeared that the insider trader was a foreigner, not local.

Before I could look at any of this, I had to become formally an employee of the Central Bank so that there would be no legal doubt as to my being able to view the transactions and act for the Central Bank. Also, as I had rather hoped, the local Swiss-owned bank had been typically Swiss in 2 respects. First, their locally-incorporated subsidiary had kept excellent records and the Central Bank man had had the sense to demand and take away from it the so-called KYC file on the client which – Swiss-style – was relatively up to date. Now, KYC stands for Know Your Customer; and it is an article of faith among bank regulators in all moderately compliant jurisdictions that each bank and share trader must know quite a lot about the client for whom they are dealing.

On this occasion, the client was a Canadian-born trader who worked on Wall Street and who had had, for years, a share trading account with this local island bank.

The records were reasonably full – including, for example photocopies of the man's current passport and his US work visa. My central bank contact confirmed what I had already suspected, namely that the local Swiss subsidiary had only 100 or so clients – a fact, together no doubt with Swiss efficiency, which meant that the records of the local firm would have been very easy to trawl when the Central Bank had called.

That was enough action for the day – at least for the Central Bank man. I agreed to return at 10 a.m. the next day to review the transactions being questioned.

Well, I won't overstate my role in what followed. Things really couldn't have been much simpler. The bank had only conducted share transactions for the trader in the documents provided, not mixed in all sorts of other banking business as well. The Swiss bank's records were meticulous. And, over the next 2 days, without undue effort, I established that this trader had bought US securities 24 times in the previous year, always selling what had been bought within 2 weeks. On 23 of the 24 occasions, the transaction had generated a profit for the trader, usually of the order of 20% or more. So, here was a man who was either remarkably percipient in monitoring the shares he dealt in or had been up to his ears in using insider information. The material supplied by the SEC to justify its demand for co-operation with the local central bank did NOT go into detail as to where the information had come from behind these transactions. And the SEC would undoubtedly need that to make their case in the US courts. But what the local record search had precipitated was an expansion of the number of insider cases – the SEC had had only had details of 15 of the 24. They could now track down the other 9. And, more to the point, in each case there was evidence to show the SEC where the cash had come from and, more importantly where the profits had been remitted. It was quite clear to me that, when the SEC got its hands on all this, the information would be of enormous help in building their whole case – possibly against a ring of insider traders.

My only regret was that the job was so quick and simple. I had been given the work on a Wednesday and, by the next Tuesday, I was back on the BA plane to London. In those few short days, I had got to know the Central Bank man well and was fairly confident that, over time, a bit more of this work might come my way – AND hopefully in the English winter. Because it's in my nature, I did ask my contact what – if anything – would be done to the local Swiss bank. The answer was very much as I had expected. *"We need banks like that here, man. They've kept their records in good order and they showed them all to us when we asked, so they've done all they need. We might suggest they are a bit more careful in future to monitor their clients' trading in New York. But they've done pretty good; and the SEC should be pretty happy with us, at least for a few months."* That, as far as he was concerned, was it. Insider trading would always be with us. It was no part of a Caribbean central bank's job to do more than make sure – if possible – that it got done elsewhere.

10

I got back to London in a better frame of mind. It's amazing what a touch of Caribbean sun can do for the spirits. That better frame even survived setting up a meeting with our lawyer (plus as many of the Management Committee as I could corral), to find out more about what the Tribunal would involve.

Our lawyer, John same name as me, always managed to hold our meetings in his office which I squared with myself on the grounds that, that way, he couldn't charge us for his travel. Not that he was a heavy charger, certainly not by comparison with our previous firm. But, when you know you will be paying for advice in 6 minute bursts (that was his – and a very common – charging model, £30 for 6 minutes in his case) you quickly came to realise how short 6 minutes was.

On this occasion, I remember that it was late afternoon when we met (easier to get Committee members to come if they could go straight home afterwards). Our lawyer had arranged his grandly-named conference room so that he sat with his back to the window and the afternoon sun poured in, illuminating the fact that he didn't have a hair on his head. We sat round and listened.

"Right, as some of you may know from last time, this Tribunal is part of the Government legal structure. There are 5 Tribunals for the country; we, of course, will be in the London one. The format is always the same. The case will be heard by 3 Assessors. The Chair will be legally qualified, the second will be a professional in the business (usually a property valuer) and the third will be a lay person. The format is supposedly informal. But Mr. U will probably have a lawyer representing him, he has had in previous cases, so it won't be that informal. You don't have to have me there. But I would certainly recommend it, unless any of you are planning on drawing up the defence and mugging up leasehold law.

Before the case starts, the Tribunal will usually try and get the conflicting parties to agree to some alternative resolution procedure – usually mediation. I think in this case they may not bother. Mediation was tried last time and it just delayed everything by 3 months to no avail. I assume none of you have a taste to try it?"
The assembled group all shook their heads.

"The lines of questioning are pretty much obvious in this case. Mr. U has identified £800k of costs that he says were unreasonable, about 30% of that being legal costs you incurred to fight him in the previous cases. In each instance, he will be out to show that the work and expense were unnecessary and/or that you didn't exercise due care in deciding who to use AND that you didn't exercise enough control to stop costs from escalating.

Now, the good news is that – where the expenditure involves regular outlays, like cleaning or security – the onus falls first on the Managing Agent to show how their procedures decided who did the work and how much to pay. That should keep some of the closest focus off you. The not so good news is that your previous Agents sound like a bunch of bozos and I believe that they've gone out of business since you got rid of them. They're not likely to be much help and that's putting it politely. But the new Agents should be able to attest that they took on clean normal commercial contracts from their predecessors.

On legal costs, again, there is good news in that the Tribunal tends to assume that legal advisers follow the rules they are supposed to follow, which should give the client a defence against things like bills just piling up. Again, given that you used what seems – from the correspondence I've seen – to be a pretty useless firm of lawyers, that may not help all that much. And, as you perhaps won't be surprised to hear, they're not keen to help us. What little part of the firm that is left is still asking £3k to put your files in order and provide a short review that you could share with the Court. I think we shall just have to argue that such a cost WOULD be unreasonable; and rely on the fact that, hopefully, Mr. U's previous brushes with the Tribunal will incline the Assessors to be sympathetic.

What else? Case is likely to take one and a half, maybe 2 days. I suggest you, John, be prepared to give evidence. You'll come across as sound and sensible, though of course you weren't around for much of the expenditure being questioned. I think you should also get your old Chairman to at least prepare a witness statement – I can help with that and leave it open until we get to the Court as whether he gives evidence if we can persuade him."

Our lawyer looked round the table, where most of the Committee seemed to have shrunk into themselves – probably thinking, not for the first time, how had they had got themselves into this? As no-one else was going to do it, I asked the one obvious remaining question. *"What happens if they find against us?" "Well"* replied our lawyer *"suppose they decide that £30k of the money was not 'reasonably spent'. Then, in theory the leaseholders can demand that money be paid back to reduce their future service charges. You, I understand it, have no reserves or fall-back money – I'm not criticising, few leaseholder associations do. Well, in short, I imagine there will be a period of chaos while Mr. U brings cases against the Management Committee that was there at the time. My guess – and it can only be that – is that he might offer to have a new leaseholders group take over the running of the bloc, one dominated by him. If he really has been doing all this to get control of the bloc, that would be game set and match to him, I'd say."*

11

Given our knowledge of leasehold law, let alone whatever arcana there were behind the term 'unreasonable expenditure', the Management Committee – when it discussed paying for our lawyer to be present – felt it had no choice but to pay for as many 6 minute packets of our lawyer's time as it would take. There were also several tense meetings of the Committee over exactly how to structure our defence, made a little less depressing by the fact that the pub landlord was now quite ready to let us have a back room in his pub, provided there was no sign of Mr. U.

Perhaps the hardest part was going back and trying to re-establish exactly what had been going on 2 or 3 years earlier. Yes, we had quite good Minutes from Committee meetings at the time. But there was very little left of either the old Managing Agent or the previous solicitor; and we were often almost totally dependent on the new Agent and solicitor to recreate a suitable backdrop explanation. Fortunately, we could – and did – take heart from the fact that much of the claimed 'unreasonable expenditure' was similar, often identical, to what the Court had ruled on previously. And, of course, on the legal bills you always had an initiating action from Mr. U. to show why costs had again been incurred. Nevertheless, it was daunting and depressing work, of which I did as much as I could to minimise our on-going legal costs.

We also talked long and hard about how to create a 'fighting fund' out of which we might be able to refund any successfully contested items. This, however, ran into the practicalities of size (how do you prepare for a bill the size of which you have no idea) and the not unreasonable view of some members that we hadn't done anything wrong, so any preparation like this looked like we had.

The given date for the Hearing arrived all too quickly. I was fortunately between jobs so could take the time off. Our lawyer and Managing Agent were both there (because they were being paid and because, indirectly, their own reputations were under attack). If I remember correctly 2 of the Committee were also there for the day and a half that the Hearing eventually took.

Looking back, I don't remember too much. The legal requirement that both sides had had to set out all their main arguments in advance meant that most of what was covered was predictable. What was new for me though was to sit about 10 yards away from Mr. U. for the day and a half and, more importantly to see and hear his lawyer. This latter gentleman was something that Charles Dickens might have conjured up, carrying with him the whiff of endless legal disputes over the years he had taken part in. The man loved the sound of his own voice, oh how he did and had a physique, especially a paunch, to go with it. And that love of his own voice was great for us because within half an hour it had got totally up the nose of the main Adjudicator. Fortunately, our Dickensian opponent was clearly not the sort to listen to hints or look at the Adjudicator's body language.

Whether the opposing lawyer was being paid by Mr. U. or whether (as I now rather think) he was part of whatever network Mr. U. had established to profit if he ever got control, there was no way of knowing. What I can say is that when on the second afternoon, after a short break, the Adjudicators gave their verdict, it came as little surprise that with the exception of one small item of expenditure (of less than £1,000 incurred before I had got on the Committee), the Tribunal found totally for us.

The whole case, of course, had cost many thousands to prepare. The tiny sum found against us was, I thought, something we could undoubtedly live with. (I remember after my third or fourth celebratory drink saying that, if need be, I'd gift it – but it fortunately never came to that.) But nevertheless a clear win. And I can recall predicting then – accurately as it turned out – that it would be a long time before Mr. U. again tried his luck with the Tribunal.

12

We got a summary of the Tribunal result out to leaseholders within 24 hours, a summary cleared, of course, at extra expense by our lawyer. For all the response we got from those leaseholders, we might as well have put round a note on a change of the rubbish collection rota. But perhaps I expect too much.

What I certainly hadn't expected was to get back from work a couple of days later and walk straight into a screaming match between Mr. U and the Head Porter. Having done so, there was nothing for it but to find out what was the problem though, to date, Mr. U and I had probably never exchanged more than 20 words.

What had happened was one of those things that always seem to occur when you don't want an awkward situation made worse. And, in this case, this was that Mr.

U had got himself trapped in a broken-down lift on the way up to his apartment.

Now the lifts in the building must have dated back I guess to the 60s or 70s. And no doubt the builders when converting the place in the 1990s had spent as little as possible in modernising them. It was certainly one of the items on the Management Committee 'to do' list to check out what it was going to cost to upgrade the lifts. But, frankly, with all the endless legal costs Mr. U was bringing and the typical lack of enthusiasm any leaseholder has to pay shared fees, we hadn't got very far on what was obviously going to be a tricky and expensive undertaking.

I think Mr. U had initially thought that somehow the Porter had engineered the snafu but even Mr. U probably thought better of that line of argument pretty quickly. By the time I got there, the argument had turned into one about how Mr. U had paid for a penthouse that was way below the standard a penthouse should be. This – the lift – was the latest evidence to support his hypothesis; but before that, as Mr. U now recited at length, was the ongoing problem of the roof and the leaks that went with it.

Again, this was something I knew a little about – and what little I did know didn't paint a totally happy picture of previous Management Committee action to sort the problem out. We ended, because I could see Mr. U was going to milk the lift for all it was worth (if you can milk a lift) and, yes, he did have a valid point, with my closing the conversation by saying I would go up on the roof in the next few days and see the situation up there for myself. With that, I swept off to my little apartment and poured myself a large G & T, leaving Mr. U and the Porter to carry on their row if they wished. I don't relish open confrontation, which had – given my past jobs – not always been avoidable. And, from my limited but now growing acquaintance with Mr. U I certainly wasn't looking for a confrontation with him. But what else could I do? Even a second G&T didn't come up with a decent answer for that.

13

It was nearly a fortnight before I did get up to that roof. In part, the delay was the result of a little spasm of work; but I also felt I needed to mug up on previous efforts to address the leaking roof, efforts which I knew had been underway for some time. And, of course, it took days for the background papers to get to me from the Managing Agent (who themselves knew little, as most of the problem had occurred on the previous Agent's watch).

The background papers didn't give much reassurance. An unkind reader would have said they just showed that superficial work had been carried out. Though I suppose it would also have been fair to say that any sizeable elderly roof is going to pose serious challenges and this was clearly no exception. No doubt the roof had had just as much expense lavished on it as the lifts during the residential conversion – i.e. as little as possible. And, of course, a 'builders' guarantee' which I found among the papers had expired about 4 years earlier – and was, in any case, in the name of what I quickly discovered was a defunct company.

I had been up on the roof once before, the day of the abseiler. And I would be the first to admit that I'm not great with heights. You got on the roof by taking the main lift to the grandly-named Penthouse Floor and opening a Fire Door onto the roof. From there, thankfully for me, there ran a thin metal pathway out to the edge of the roof and all the way round the roof. Along a good part of the walkway ran a metal rail at hand height so that when (every few yards) I started to worry about vertigo, I could at least hold onto something.

About the only other good thing I could find to say was that ours wasn't the tallest building in the area, so I could – by looking out – see the rooves, usually flat, of buildings around us. An illusion of course but something that I could turn into the idea that I wasn't several hundred feet in the air and that there was terra firma around me. The only place where this didn't work was when one got to the edge of the roof. There, a steep run of roofing tiles ran about 4 yards down to an elaborate balustrade which one of the papers I'd found doing my homework had described. Apparently the artwork of the balustrade, if you could call such a thing artwork, was made primarily of lead and, worse, was protected by some local authority preservation order as being 'typical of high Art Deco building work'. If you peered further beyond the balustrade, which I wasn't keen to do, you could see what looked like a precipitate and immediate drop to the ground far below.

As for the roof itself, which I had gone up to view, the picture looked pretty grim. Asphalt covered by varying but usually low levels of shingle; and an awful lot of roof none of which seemed newer or better protected than the rest. I wondered around for a few minutes, in splendid isolation. I came to a halt outside the picture window of one of the 5 penthouse flats and gazed rather blankly in. On one level, the penthouses didn't have much – certainly not any kind of view, panoramic or otherwise. But, I mused, if you'd paid a good deal more I could see that you'd hardly be amused by having your ceiling and window surrounds leak. I had some vague notion that penthouses typically went for around 20% more than property without that title; whatever the figure was here, it wasn't buying much.

I snapped out of my reverie, looking through this window, when an all too familiar figure rose seemingly out of nowhere inside the penthouse. Just my luck, I had picked Mr. U's flat and he was at home. We stood looking at each other for about 10 seconds and then I could hear a torrent of what could only be abuse coming from inside. I could catch the phrase '*spying* on me' but otherwise nothing. The English language and culture doesn't have much to deal with a situation like that. I remember smiling rather inanely and waving my hands around in the general direction of the roof. I seemed to remember having told him I would *come* up to the roof and have a look. Well, here I was.

After about 20 seconds of pantomime gestures (and further abuse) from inside the flat, Mr. U suddenly changed tactics. His hands shot in the air, he turned and charged away from the window. I started to move on, walking away from his window, which inevitably meant towards the nearest edge of the roof. About 45 seconds later there he was, bursting out of the same Fire Door I had used and walking very purposefully towards me in my new location.

"I have come to see what your problems with the roof are" I called. He stopped in mid-stride and seemed to mull that over. *"No you haven't"* he screeched. *"You've come to spy on me. You and your wretched Committee."* A good deal more followed this but I must confess not to remembering what. He may have been talking in Russian or some other language. Or it may be I was just a bit shell-shocked. Anyway, I did what was probably the worst thing I could have done and turned my back on him. I looked down; my brain was reminding me that I was alone, several hundred feet in the air and with a large and decidedly unhappy man shouting at me.

The rest happened in less than a minute, I guess. I had just reached a point near the edge of the roof where the little walkway turned a corner to follow the roof along. Mr. U, behind me, must have charged at me – I remember turning and seeing him within a couple of yards of me. I slipped and fell on the asphalt. He, arms wheeling and still shouting incoherently, rushed past – indeed over me. His paunch hit the low metal railing which turned at that point as did the walkway itself; and he executed a rather ungraceful slow motion somersault over the railing. That brought him directly onto the sloping tiles at the edge of the roof. From my very poor vantage point on the floor, I lost sight of him. But I did hear a shout and a large thud, then silence.

I'm afraid I didn't cover myself in glory. I was promptly sick on the asphalt which was now an inviting 6 inches from my chin and fainted!

14

I came to in an ambulance; and, although I had never been in one, it was somehow obvious to me that an ambulance was where I was. A middle-aged paramedic was sitting to my right. When he saw I was awake he gave a fleeting smile (I guess such people don't have many reasons to smile and so probably don't do too much of it) and said *"Don't worry mate, you're on the way to somewhere that can take a proper look at you. Bit of advice. Next time you faint, do try and make sure you're somewhere easier to get to; getting you down on a stretcher from that roof wasn't the easiest thing I'll do today. Though I have to say that compared with the other guy who seemed to have tried to throw himself off the roof, I suppose things could have been worse. I'll be hearing about that from my colleague later, no doubt."*

I deduced from that typically leaden bit of British humour that I couldn't be in too much danger. Otherwise, surely it would just have been a minimalist *"Don't worry we're getting you seen to."* But also it brought a flood of painful memories back. Where was Mr U? What had happened? I thought I knew that there was a further short balcony about 10 feet down below the main balustrade, so if he had gone over the edge there had to be a good chance that he had been saved by that, even though it would still have been a very nasty fall. My brain was scrambled but I couldn't recall hearing the sort of cry one typically associated with someone falling a long way. But maybe he'd knocked himself unconscious on the way? Supposing he had gone over the balustrade? Next stop would be street level, a long way down.

Lying there in the ambulance, I didn't feel good. My heart seemed to be jumping on a trampoline. And one of the mental tricks I normally used to do when I wanted to make sure that I was awake failed miserably, which seemed to me a sure sign something was wrong.

What's that trick you ask? Well, it was something I picked up years ago when I was a foreign exchange dealer; and apparently it's also one of the tests back long ago that President Reagan said he would undergo from time to time to prove he wasn't senile. Perhaps we could try it on some of our older politicians, or perhaps on Trump. Anyway, the trick is to count down quickly from 100 in 7s, 9s or 11s. Suppose you choose 11s. If you can come up in your head with 100, 89, 78, 67… or whatever – quickly and without stumbling there's not too much wrong with you. On this occasion I did it in 7s and after

93 I had to admit to myself I was stuck. I couldn't ever remember having had a problem with this trick before.

I don't remember much of my time in the hospital they took me to – St Edwards' I think it was. Lots of serious faced and rather tired people prodding at me, conducting ECGs (electrocardiograms if you don't know) and God knows what else; and then hitching me up to machines whose purpose seemed primarily to make sure I couldn't move without setting off a mechanical alarm of some kind. I'm sure they talked to me about what they were doing; but I just wasn't in receiving mode. It all washed over me, though I did pick up enough to gather that my heart wasn't in as good a shape as it ought to be at my age.

I had gone into hospital, I suppose about 3 pm. They had done most of what they were obviously going to do by about 8pm. And then the night. This was far worse than the day because most of us in the ward were plugged into these machines but there weren't nearly enough staff to do anything about the alarms that regularly went off. So, that night consisted of little more than endless alarms going off and being ignored by the 2 night nurses assigned to guard us; I use the word 'guard' advisedly. Sleep was impossible in the circumstances. My only other memory is from the one time I was able to escape the embrace of the machines and go to the loo. I took the chance to look around. My memory? The notice on a board for staff – and I only remember that because it was in Polish. Heaven help the NHS. Heaven help us.

The next morning, hospital routine began again in earnest. Shift changeover at some ungodly hour, a bit of breakfast and then various groups (presumably young trainees) coming round to look at us, led in most cases by one older and presumably qualified person. When 2 people came and sat down by my bed, having drawn the privacy curtains round first, my initial thought was that this was another of those groups. That illusion was shattered by them both pulling badges from their pockets and introducing themselves as Metropolitan police! I realised instantly that no-one had said a word all this time about Mr. U. Worse, I hadn't asked.

I didn't say anything. The woman, who was clearly the senior of the 2, broke the silence. *"Mr. Carter?"* "Yes" I replied *"what do you want?" "We're here, Sir, to find out a bit more what happened on that roof yesterday. Take your time but just tell us in your own words."*

"Well" I said *"Very simple really. I got the key to the roof from the porter and went out onto the roof about 2.30 pm I guess. As you probably know, I'm the Chairman of the Management Committee and I wanted to have a proper look at the state of the roof and also the balustrade. I've only ever been up there briefly before. Well, it certainly looks like we're going to have to spend a lot of money sorting some of the problems; and it also looks as though the money already spent up there has been spent to very little effect. But, as I say, I just wanted to get a feel for the scale of the problem before our next Management Committee meeting.*

Anyway, there I am. I'm going round the roof and, when I get opposite Mr. Uranishi's penthouse window, there he is suddenly, standing looking out. He sees me, and starts shouting at me through his window."

"What was he saying?" the woman asked. *"To be honest, it wasn't very clear"* I said. *"I don't think English is*

his native language and he seemed angry. I heard something about people's privacy and that I was a spy; and I think then something about how the state of the roof was a disgrace. I have to say I rather agree with that last point. I was rather surprised to see Mr. Uranishi at all if I'm honest. It hadn't crossed my mind that he would be there. The last thing I'd heard was that he had rented out the flat to some Russians. But, there he was. Anyway, I listened to the tirade for a minute –I didn't respond, I couldn't really hear it properly – I've always felt that to get dragged into arguments like that helps no-one. I just turned to get on with my inspection. About 45 seconds later, there he is behind me on the roof, having come out of the Fire Door. I guess he'd just rushed out of his apartment and round to the door leading onto the roof. He was still shouting and generally looked furious. Again, I didn't respond – it still seemed that was the best option. It was all rather embarrassing, even if no-one else was around. I don't like confrontations. I thought the best thing would be to find another route back to the door, round the roof, and avoid anything further.

So, I turned to look for a dignified way to get out. I heard a bellow from Mr Uranishi behind me. I think he said something like 'don't turn your back on me, I have rights'. But that may be just my imagination. Next thing, I knew, I turned back to face *him and he was charging the 10 yards or so gap between us. Well, if you've seen him you'll know he's quite – how shall I say – substantial. A good 3 or 4 inches taller than me and stones heavier. Fortunately I was standing somewhere where I had already stepped safely to one side and he just carried on past me. I think I had slipped down by this time. The next thing I knew, he has gone over the little railing at a speed of knots, lurched forward and I couldn't see him anymore. That's when I had my heart attack or whatever it was. The next thing I really know I woke up in the ambulance. What actually happened?"*

My two visitors looked at each other. *"Well"* said the woman *"Mr Uranishi did indeed fall over the railing – you'll recall it's only about waist height. But, fortunately for him, he went fair and square into the balustrade. I understand he has broken his left arm and a couple of ribs – and taken a very nasty blow on the head. But, all in all, it could have been hugely worse."*

"That's something" I replied. The female officer went on. *"The problem, Sir, not to put too fine a point on it, is that Mr. Uranishi is saying that you grabbed him as he went passed you and that you either tripped him or pushed him (he's not very clear about which – that may just be the bang on his head). He's demanding that we investigate. And, as what he describes could amount to Grievous Bodily Harm, I'm afraid we have no choice but to do so. We've come now to have a preliminary word. We will be talking to anyone who might have heard your altercation and, of course, our forensic people are combing over the roof. With that in mind, we'd like to take away the clothes you were wearing for a forensic review. Your doctor here says you won't be going anywhere for a few days. I hope by then we can take a formal statement from you and establish what, if anything more, needs to be done. "*

I just lay there – two hammer blows. The first being Uranishi's crazy allegations – obviously vindictive nonsense but how was I going to prove that? We'd been up there on our own. The second blow as the 'you won't be going anywhere, Sir'. That was considerably more (and worse) than anything the docs had said to me. Naively, I had imagined, any time soon, they would have been letting me out, to go home. But seemingly not.

The police were obviously waiting for me to say something. Something clicked into action in my head. *"Yes"* I said *"Of course you can have my clothes. But do please find out what you can about Mr. Uranishi. A lot of people in the bloc will be able to tell you about some of his history; and do please talk to our solicitor about the legal dance he has been doing with us over the last few years. I had absolutely nothing to do with him getting injured."*

That seemed to satisfy them. The woman nodded, said *"Thank you"* and they left.

15

I suppose in one way I could thank Mr U. For, after the police had gone, I realised I would have 2 things to worry – my health and the police investigations, not just the former. In fact, the next 3 days were something of a blur in my memory. On the health front, the number and apparent seniority of the medical staff who came to see me went up several notches, which did my mood little good. They never said much – certainly nothing of any use. But I was trundled off for various x-rays. And, the one substantive thing I do recall, they took me off and shoved something called a stent up me to look – they said – at the chambers of my heart. Nothing painful. But a very odd sensation, having a long tube inserted somewhere at hip level and then being able to look – with the doctors – at a television screen showing my heart as the stent was moved around.

I had a welcome visitor – I think on the third day – Frank from the Management Committee and the leaseholder I had always got on best with. [I had already realised what a drawback it was/would be not to have family members able to drop in and undertake at least a few simple things for me while I was flat on my back.] Frank seemed in remarkably high spirits. God knows what stories were circulating back at the bloc. Certainly, I hoped nothing that the police would pick up and misuse. But Frank had been alerted to my whereabouts by the Head Porter; and the porter was clearly playing the whole thing as a story of 'How Mr. U had got his comeuppance.'

I listened to what Frank had to say and then spent 20 minutes trying to inject a bit of reality into his story. So at least he could understand what had actually happened. I was also able to give him a couple of phone numbers, so that my family could at least be alerted to my position (I had my mobile phone with me but somehow the idea of ringing my ex-wife and explaining what had happened was more than I could face.) And I was able also give him my flat keys – the police had at least left those with me – so that he could return the next day with some more clothing and shoes for me. Whatever the police had said, I didn't want to be stuck in the hospital without clothing if it turned out that I could go home. Frank was delighted to help – I knew he didn't have too much to do in his normal daily round. And he left promising clothes and books, plus some fruit and chocolate the next day.

The police returned a day later than Frank – I think it was a day but it could have been 2. The same couple as before, who sat in the same chairs as before and, again, with the woman doing the talking. The man produced his notepad and the woman began with a short, no doubt pre-rehearsed, speech.

"We've been pretty busy, Mr. Carter. We found 2 other penthouse leaseholders who heard at least something of the altercation – one of them actually looked out and saw a bit of it. It was him who got the ambulance. Our Forensic people have looked at your and Mr. Uranishi's clothing and at the roof. And we are of the opinion that, what few hard facts there are, are consistent with your version of events. The leaseholders both heard Mr Uranishi shouting but not your good self, which fits with your version. The place on the roof where you say you moved out of his way suggests that you did, as you said, end up falling as you moved out of his way. Most importantly, there is no DNA evidence on either set of clothes that you laid hands on Mr. Uranishi or he on you (he now says he did grapple with you) or that you were close to him when he went over the railing.

You will be pleased to learn that we are closing the investigation unless anything further comes to light. You may also be pleased to know that, if Mr. Uranishi takes any private legal action against you (which he says he intends to do), all the information we have established will be available to you should you wish. Your clothes and shoes will be retained for a further month. But, apart from my colleague here working through with you a short witness statement that we have taken the liberty of drawing up after our earlier visit, I'm pleased to say our interest is now at an end."

At that point the woman left. The young male officer took over and very calmly talked me through the statement they had prepared for me. I have to say it was pretty good. We agreed a handful of changes. He then disappeared, had it retyped; and I signed off later that afternoon, when he returned. That, thank Heavens, was the last I saw of them. And the need to call for their evidence, later, never materialised as Mr. U never brought any action against me. But that's jumping the gun. Let me finish the story in the proper order.

16

I suppose I was in St. Edwards for another week; but time was pretty blurry at that point. My ex-wife and one of the children came in to see me, which was a nice if somewhat odd way to reconnect with them. I promised myself I would do better by them in future, as and when I got the chance. Frank popped in a couple of times too; but, otherwise, the residents of The House were noticeable by their absence. If you disappear from view in the City between 6pm on Friday night and 8am Monday morning, the culture is clear. 'The dogs bark and the caravan moves on' as one 1930s Governor of the Bank of England is supposed to have said. Certainly, there's nowhere easier than the City to disappear like that; and everyone else is too busy – and too scared of the same thing happening to them – to do anything about it.

The medics seemed to become increasingly concerned about me , though I guess to be fair that was me interpreting what they were saying, as much as what they actually said. Now I'm much further down the medical chain, as it were, I have concluded that doctors find it almost impossible to offer an objective, warts and all, summary of your position at any point in the process. Yes, they do spell out the risks of what they recommend (and, usually in censorious tones, what they think will happen if you ignore their recommendations). But there is also always a seemingly forced measure of rosy scenario in everything they do tell you. What they don't say – which is what I now think was the honest position with me – is *'Look, Mr. Carter. Your heart is knackered. We'll do what we can but the operation is risky; and, at best, you'll never get back to where you were before this all blew up.'*

Anyway, to cut the *story* to the minimum, they moved me from St. Edwards to Harefield the premier heart hospital in London I'm told. There I met the surgeon who was going to operate; and he was refreshingly a bit more honest. *"Your heart's in a bad way"* he said. *"We're going to do a 3 or 4 valve bypass and see if that does the trick. It's really the only option but I think it will work. You'll need to plan on being on your back for a fortnight, first in intensive care and then mostly laid up for another 6-8 weeks while your chest starts to mend and we get you onto a series of remedial exercises. After that, too soon to say. But, whatever you are planning by way of preparation, best get on with it. Your heart is going downhill quite fast. I want to operate in 3 to 4 days."*

For my own sake, I'll fill in the rest quickly. (It still hurts to think about what caused the giant scar on my chest that –even after 6 years – I still think of as an opening post-mortem cut come early). They did a 4 valve bypass; and the surgeon's predictions about the immediate post-operative period were broadly confirmed. He did a great job. By any realistic measure, I've now got a good quality of life and I don't go to bed each night half expecting the ticker to give up on me before morning. But all the rest, like the consultation work and a reasonably easy retirement, that's all up in smoke, though I got out with enough cash that I can live well out of London and not particularly well, if you see what I mean; in short, I manage.

What I do want to describe briefly – because I think how well it shows the overall and lasting effect Mr. U has had on me – was the screw up that occurred the night after my operation. Again, I'll be brief as these are not happy memories. To keep the pain at bay, they must have pumped me full of morphine and other goodies. Whatever the exact mixture, it had a bizarre effect; and, when I awoke after the operation, I started having seriously bad hallucinations. The operation had lasted 6 hours. All I knew, when I woke up, were 2 things. First, I had seen Mr. U and, second, cats and dogs were running up and down the curtains. (Plus the fact that this state of affairs didn't seem to worry me much.)

I'm sure now that seeing Mr U was a complete illusion. But he was obviously uppermost in my mind as I struggled out of my operation. And my picture of him was so real. I had been lying in my bed and, opposite me were several men lying in beds too. What I thought I saw was Mr. U was walking up and down the row opposite, talking to some of the men in the beds – with his back to me. And he was photographing the men. No-one told me but I just knew that these were the men he had been using to claim fake whiplash injuries.

I just sank into my bed and hoped not to be noticed. And that seemed to be working until – just as I think he was about to leave – Mr U turned and saw me. A frown crossed his face and then a look of recognition. He came towards me – I was lying there helpless and, I now saw that I was attached to several large machines. I couldn't move. *"Well, Mr Carter"* he said. *"This is a rather different set up from The House isn't it? But I see that – as with there – you're still being a bloody nuisance. Must be time I think for me to help you on your way."* He grinned from ear to ear and lent forward – as I saw it to do something to one of the machines I was hooked up to. I was helpless.

There was nothing I could do, no nurse or anyone there to help me. At that point in my dream and just as he was reaching out to one of my machines – I fainted or fell asleep again.

When I came to, I was pretty hysterical – or, at least that is how it must have appeared to the staff. *"Where is he?"* I can remember shouting *"He's going to kill me."*

I've very little idea of what then happened, other than – about 24 hours later – something like normality had been restored. The cats and dogs had disappeared. They must have 'sorted' my drug overload. I felt normal, if completely exhausted and demoralised can be described as 'normal'. At some point, presumably sometime then, a doctor must finally have explained that I had had 'post operative disorder – POD'. This, it turns out, is quite common for older people undergoing major surgery. And, no, they didn't think to warn any poor sod like me beforehand that such things could happen.

No doubt, for them, that drew the curtain on what must have been an awkward event for them, let alone for me. What I DO remember very vividly from that point on, is resolving to sell out of the bloc as quickly as I could and never to do anything again about the Management Committee, leasehold law or Mr. U. And that is what I've done. For all I know, Mr. U, Frank and the lawyer are still all there peering across court rooms or tables at each other. I certainly can't believe that peace and harmony have broken out there or that there has been a particularly happy ending for anyone. I'm just grateful that I got out with most of my money intact from the sale of the flat; and that my heart – freed now of the fear of walking round a corner into Mr. U or trouble of any other kind – is still functioning well enough to keep me going.

17

I don't think I ever said '*the world's my* oyster' when I was young. Not because I wasn't hugely, irrationally optimistic in those days. Quite the contrary. Everyday I was learning and – I thought – improving my position in the world. Everyday, science was improving mankind's lot. There was nothing that, between us, the new and coming generation couldn't sort out. No, the simple reason was that I have always disliked oysters. It would never have occurred to me to use the phrase.

Now, like almost any older person, I feel less sanguine than I did. Humanity has certainly notched up some impressive pluses in my life. The worst forms of poverty have been reduced, life expectancy has risen, new technology has made some amazing things not just possible but humdrum. But for each one of these advances you can find a negative as big. The world's climate and environment is shot to pieces – that's probably the worst I can think of. And, to echo the theme of my own little story, the real problem is that nowhere do I see the general will or understanding to take the measures that would be needed to make any worthwhile difference to deal with the problem of greed. Most people are – as they always have been – greedy, short-sighted and always looking for an 'out' that cuts – preferably avoids altogether – the costs to them.

My mood swings by the day. When I'm down, I reflect on the kind of examples that show just what we're up against if we are to change human nature. Some of them are 'big', ones you might think of yourself. For example, 9/11. This scores on 2 grounds; first that terrorists could do such a thing to kill so many innocent people; and then, second, because so many people afterwards came up with crazy stories about Mossad or the US itself setting up the strikes.

Some of the others on my list are sports-related – not surprising given how much sport I've followed over the years. Things like Michael Tyson chewing off part of the ear of an opponent – NOT because he did it but because he was allowed to continue afterwards as a professional fighter, too much of a box-office star to be banned. On a smaller scale, the professional rugby player who faked a blood injury (complete with blood brought onto the field for the purpose) so he could be replaced by someone more suitable. That makes my list because – innocent that I am – I had previously thought that, if any sport were free of such jiggery-pokery, it would be rugby union.

The list grows I should note. Just this week (July 2019) an addition because Boris Johnson visited a sausage factory as part of his quest to become Prime Minister. Within hours, the firm's website was inundated with unfavourable views on the firm's sausages. A sad vindictive little effort that earned a place on my list – reviews made by a bunch of people who can clearly make no distinction between politics and sausages.

When I'm more cheerful, my thoughts typically run in better channels. I think of someone who died say in 1919, when the flu epidemic had just killed more people even than the First World War. Or a British soldier killed at Dunkirk. Life at both times must have seemed deeply, deeply, desperate; and yet, in time, these things passed and were replaced by 'better'.

I'm also often comforted by, of all things, a science-fiction story I can remember reading in the 1970s. A man is time transported to a parallel universe and plonked down in what is obviously the front line of a battle. The side he is on, purely by dint of having been dropped there, is made up of normally rational people. But they have been panicked by being attacked by an army led by a giant baby whose movements the opposing army controls with prods and restraints. Our rational 'modern man' sees this and points out to his 'side' that all they have to do is arrange a huge fright for the baby, at which point it is likely to go beserk and destroy most of the other army. His side set up a giant 'ghost' with huge sheets and noise that appears in front of the baby; which then duly panics, destroys its constraints and stamps on most of its army. The bit I most liked though – because it seemed so true to life – was the fact that as soon as normality has been restored, the good burghers who have won turned on the modern man who had helped them. They now said that they could and would in time have seen what needed to be done. The modern man really hadn't done anything at all.

So, there are good days and bad. All you have to do to find out which I was having is to ask me about Mr. U. If I say I feel he is waiting for me outside my little room, you knew to ask no more. He spent quite a few days out there waiting for me in my mind, though thank God I never again saw him.

This has been a story firmly set in the Noughties and in the City of London. It hasn't been about the people at the top of the ant heap, most of whom generally came out OK – and nearly always do. It is about people like me, a good bit further down the ant heap. The sort of people who would smile tiredly at the old crack (because it described them all too closely for comfort) that they were like mushrooms at work; kept in the dark and covered regularly with manure.

I've given up hoping that 'good will win in the end' or any such platitude. George Orwell's ending to 1984 seems to me the much more plausible eventual outcome for us all. I do hope, though, that some of the messages of my little tale have resonance – and not just for this particular time and place. There wouldn't have been much point in sharing it with you, otherwise. History isn't much use unless it teaches the reader something about human frailties and strengths; and it should help future generations learn from the mistakes of their forebears. You don't have to make the mistakes for yourself to learn – though sometimes it feels like that is all too often how it turns out.

What I'm trying to get across is that any social/political system – if it is not policed properly – will generate greed and 'bad behaviour'. I think what was most wrong with us in all the Noughties was that those in charge opened doors to 'entrepreneurship' and risk-taking wherever they could but failed to keep tabs on what they let in through those doors. They forgot that a lot of people are financial innocents and, indeed, that those who are not are often by nature pretty greedy. On top of that, they promised to let the risk-takers keep any rewards obtained, while tidying away any big financial disasters leaving the taxpayer – like the wretched Irish – to pay and sort them out. In a world like that, of course the pigs will always get their noses in the trough. In the Noughties, there were no serious penalties for those at the top if they cheated or if they failed; and for years there seemed to be an awful lot of pigswill to go round for all.

But very little of this was new. What we saw up to and during the Global Financial Crisis had just the same roots as any number of earlier economic crises in different parts of the world. All these crises have the letters **P.I.G** stamped all the way through them, like seaside rock. If the next generation wants to do better, it needs to root out (pig similes are so easy when you start) and identify what is the P I and G in any situation.

P.I.G? Just a reminder. Prejudice, Ignorance and Greed, the 3 major ingredients of every financial stupidity I have ever witnessed or read about, like the ones covered here. **Prejudice**: that can be as simple as preferring an American company over the French competitor just because of where they are based or because of what Mr. Trump wants. Or it can be incredibly subtle and seemingly based on reams of research, such as the now infamous (and largely useless) company ratings on new types of securities issued by the major ratings companies in the run up to the GFC. (Remember CLOs, CLO squareds and all the rest of the sub-prime rubbish – nearly all of which carried what at the time were seen as assurances of due diligence and credit worthiness by the leading rating agencies.)

Ignorance, likewise, can be found almost everywhere. We are all – bound to be – ignorant about many things. I, for example, will freely admit I have no idea how a nuclear power station works. The important point, though, is that I shouldn't run or in any way have anything to do with such a power station. Probably best if I don't invest in it or have any other financial dealings involving it. Ignorance is inevitable. The important thing is to admit it when it's there.

Greed, finally, is probably by far the worst problem, the yeast without which few financial scams rise so far and so fast. Of course one could plausibly argue that some element of greed is necessary to make any economic system – and certainly a capitalist system – work. But, if we are to make any progress in future as capitalists, in avoiding at least the worst of the avoidable economic disasters, we need to find some better way of getting at least a few of the basics across to the next generation.

It wouldn't be a bad place to start to try and do that by memorising and trying to follow the 3 simple statements that most of my many years of economics theory boiled down to.

Statement 1: **there is no such thing as a free lunch**. The lunch won't be free – one way or another there will be strings attached, and you will find those strings jerked when you least want. That's true if you agree to attend a 'no strings' timeshare presentation. It's equally true when you use the browser offered by your IT provider, unless the regulators are a great deal more awake and with it than they usually are.

Statement 2**: if it looks to be too good to be true, it IS too good to be tr**ue. Remember my crocodile story. Next time you see that financial ad that guarantees you an astronomic return, ask yourself whether the plan is (a) illegal (illegality could certainly bring high returns) (b) guaranteed by someone whose guarantee is probably worthless when push comes to shove or (c) based on mathematical assumptions that would shame a primary school child.

Statement 3 and probably the hardest to adhere to: **don't throw good money after bad**. That roulette wheel may have come up red 10 times in a row. The odds that the next throw will also be red are still basically 50:50 (if you ignore the zero).

All my 'PIG' imagery is a bit tough on pigs themselves, I suppose. I don't know where or when pigs got a bad human press but they've had it for a long time. Apparently, they are actually clever and fairly clean animals. But, apart from the odd exception, like PG Wodehouse's Empress of Blandings – pigs don't ever have much good said for them. And it seems to be true that, if hungry, pigs will eat almost anything. Perhaps it's their cleverness that worries us – as it certainly seemed to worry George Orwell in Animal Farm, or Margaret Attwood when she dreamed up piggoons. Or perhaps pigs are just a bit too like us, especially when they appear on our TV screen dressed as a politician or a financier?

Whatever the reasons, we are left with the term 'pigswill' to describe their food. That word can be – and is readily – used as a term of abuse for food. But perhaps we should be breaking the word up. You can do a Lynn Truss on the word. Is it p**ig swill**? Or has it a rather different meaning, '**pigs will**…' as in 'pigs will always do what they do.' Like 'follow the money' in some who-dunnit, the message I leave you is this. If you identify the prejudice, ignorance and greed involved in any economic situation, you'll be more than half-way to avoid getting hurt in it. But accept that there will always be a willing supply of pigs trying to get to the trough.

THE FOUR WINDS

1

World Health was a company that didn't cover much more than the UK. But its name change from 'British Health' came in a period in which companies changed name with abandon, often becoming a little mysterious in the process. This was roughly when BA ceased to stand for British Airways and BP soon ceased to stand for British Petroleum. And a switch from 'British' to 'World' did at least reflect the ambitions of those in charge of WH at the time. But it did nothing of itself to change the company, which a British stockbroker at the time might have identified as a sizeable UK firm just big enough to be in the FTSE 100, with a main line of business in insurance in the UK and a collection of other assets acquired along the way.

From the point of view of WH, that description was not particularly comfortable. The corporate waters they now swam in meant either that you ate or were eaten; and, truth to tell, they were big enough to eat but not readily able to eat anything of size that might strengthen their own position significantly. The executives by and large enjoyed their present status and certainly didn't want to be swallowed by some global insurance player. So, from 2016, the search was on at WH for a way of obtaining more capital, so as to become big enough to eat something sizeable, This, ideally, would be a firm with an insurance business of its own in Europe or North America (to limit competition issues).

The other obvious component of any major re-jig – at least to the reigning CEO, Marcus Fox and the City – was how WH could monetise the various non-insurance assets it had acquired. Suitably organised, this would help – with a rights issue thrown in – to finance a takeover bid if one could be found. Top of those assets was a collection of Care Homes, Retirement Villages and related ventures that WH had acquired over many years. The Retirement sector had been through its own traumas, not least the very public and prolonged collapse of the largest single corporate provider of Care Homes a couple of years earlier. (But then, if you pay yourselves dividends financed out of high-interest borrowing, the result is rarely likely to be pretty; and that had certainly been the case with this provider.)

The economics of the sector had also come under a serious cloud, because successive Governments were pushing up the tiny National Minimum wages on which most Care Homes employees existed. And, overall, wages typically took up 70% of costs. At the same time, Local Authorities – who ended up paying for many of the residents (certainly after the residents' own funds had run out) – were proving more and more reluctant to go on financing further fee increases. Finally, after the Brexit referendum, the top end of the housing market in the South East went into hibernation. Elderly couples who were thinking of downsizing from Kensington or Islington suddenly found it harder to make large paper profits on the downsizing and typically pulled back (well, the elderly are usually fairly cautious). That hit the top of the retirement market just as lower down was feeling the effects of the wage increases and the lack of local authority funding.

Anyway, by the late 2010s, people like Marcus Fox could only reasonably conclude that making money out of the elderly was no easy matter, even if once it might have been. And the problems firms faced – rising wages at the bottom end of the labour market, vanishing numbers of nurses which could be made far worse if the EU-Brexit negotiations went wrong, a weak housing market – looked set to stay.

So, Fox frequently found himself chewing over how it might be possible to repackage what was a sizeable chunk of residential property (their 200 or so care homes and Retirement Villages), in a way that would allow WH to exit with cash for its stake, to use in a take-over. Fox certainly hoped his advisors could come up with something; he had not. His corporate honeymoon when he was appointed CEO had effectively run out now that he was more than a year in office. He needed a deal, a large one; and it was increasingly becoming a case of any deal would do, if it was big enough and could be packaged by the PR people as 'exciting and novel'.

2

'Might have beens' are usually not worth spending much time thinking about after the event. And it might indeed have been that WH's city advisors would eventually have come up with what Fox needed. But, as luck would have it, Fox made his own good fortune when, in 2017, he decided that a CEO of a firm like WH should appear at the Annual World Economic Forum Conference of the great and the good in Switzerland, near the end of January. This was where the Trumps, the Mays, the Macrons were to be found for a week, rubbing shoulders with the mightiest corporate names. Surely WH –or, more precisely Marcus Fox – should be with them? Or so he reasoned.

Fox nearly changed his mind after the WH press people had explained what was involved. Unless you were a Trump, what you could access at the WEF depended solely on what you or your company paid for. An all-areas (white) pass would cost up to $500,000 for the 5 days. Most of the 2,500 or so participants paid less but then tried to ensure that their names would be on some of the big rollers' 'to see' list, so that they actually got to some worthwhile events.

As the PR girl put it to Fox. *"Look, the World Economic Forum is unique. It started in 1971 on the basis of bringing the political and business great and the good together, in a small alpine retreat where they could rub shoulders for a few days in a relaxed atmosphere. Now, it's so big, it'll take you one visit just to find out how it all works and how to get something out of it. But there will be a lot of CEOs like you around, working the circuit on a corporate subscription. Most of the global players in insurance will be represented. There are always loads of conference sessions on different aspects of insurance – I hear one of the themes slated this time is 'Artificial Intelligence in insurance'. And the big pharma companies will be there; they'll be only too keen to track you down and entertain you.*

WH needs to pay for a fixer who will make sure that those big boys interested in you get to know you are going. Our firm can find you one of those. This will get you invites to some of the more fancy parties, which tend to be in private chateaux rather than the big hotels. Otherwise, it is a question of sitting round at the Conference Centre listening to well-meaning but generally insubstantial seminars on the issues of the day, as chosen by the play-makers that year. Most of the big hitters typically drop into at least a couple of sessions. So, if you have ever wanted to meet Jeff Bezos or whoever, you have your chance.

As Fox's PR advisor explained, none of this came without effort. Once you had got your pass, the first thing to do was to drop a line to all the CEOs and others you thought might be going or who probably wanted to go. Those who weren't going would be duly impressed by the fact that you were. For those who were going, there was always the chance of an invite for you to something – your rivals want to *"show off just as much as you do".* The PR girl promised that Fox's fixer would co-ordinate the diary for the few days – an extra expense, but you needed someone who understood the timing and ins and outs of WEF life. Arriving somewhere 20 minutes before Donald Trump was due at the same place could ruin your evening before it started.

It usually worked out the girl said, certainly would do in a second year once you had established in the first year how the circus was run. Her only other advice was to make sure you arranged a few suitable snap shots (cost again additional but anything – as the PR girl stressed – could be bought there if you had the money). Your fixer would also arrange personal media coverage to get the odd shot of you with the great and the good. But, she added as something of an afterthought, you don't get much of Trump in 30 seconds. However, it didn't matter even if the great and the good had no idea who you were; and now, with photoshopping, you really only needed to be in the same room as your target for 10 minutes for your 'advisor' to produce a suitable record of meeting a few great men. *"Just do it"* she said. *"You want people to think you had a great time –it doesn't really matter if you did or not. It's what your social media says afterwards that counts."*

3

When Fox actually got to the WEF in early 2018, the extent of the hard work hit him quickly, as did the sheer loneliness of the whole process. His diary boasted a dozen or so events per day. But at least half of these were conference sessions at the Congress Centre where all and sundry might be present. Another piece of advice his fixer had provided was that he needed to 'go with the flow'. Some of the best things happened almost spontaneously he'd been told repeatedly. And the days could be very long she had warned. As she put it "*Be careful if you use uppers. Pop a pill or two during the day if you must; but* remember *you may have to keep going til 4 a.m. There are always a good few photos in the press after the event of somebody face down on the hotel floor. If you end up in one of those photos, don't expect us to help. You'll have to explain it to your Board all by yourself.*"

Fox had some things to be grateful for. He had a decent hotel room about 10 minutes snow and slush away from the Congress Centre, where the biggest semi-public events happened. And Mrs Fox had mercifully shown no sign of interest when he had raised the fact that WH needed him to be there. Fortunately, he didn't feel the cold and had packed carefully. So the mild snow outside and the overwarm hotel interiors he navigated with ease. What he found much more stressful was the need to press endless flesh around every conference gathering, try to find out who the hell he was talking to and then move on as quickly as he decently could, if they were of no relevance. Half of it was automatic. His business card proffered in the left hand as his right-hand shook the hundredth hand of the day, the little quick mutual evaluation of what each of your business cards said and then on, or not.

But it wasn't really him. And, by the middle of the third day, he was ready to drop. If his wife had walked up to him at that point, he realised with a start that he would probably have shaken her firmly by the hand and said *"Hi, I'm Marcus Fox of WH; and your line of business?"* Instead, the hundredth hand that day actually turned into a face that smiled at him and said *"Good to have found you, Mr. Fox I've been looking for you. Frank Brightwell is the name, CFO for Liford Private Equity which you may have heard of. Let's get out of this noise and confusion so I can introduce myself properly."*

One of the features of the WEF seemed to be that nowhere indoors seemed more than 30 yards away from carefully drawn-up chairs and a nearby coffee station.

Brightwell threw himself into the first suitable chair and smiled again over at Fox. *"I've had as much coffee as my system can take but don't let me stop* you." Fox said he too would pass.

Brightwell proved an engaging and easy listener. He seemed to know quite a lot about WH (Fox had found that perhaps two-thirds of the people he had spoken to over the 3 days didn't even know what WH was). He also seemed genuinely interested in Fox himself and was quite open – when asked – about his own life and activities.

After about half an hour, Brightwell looked at his watch and – breaking the chain of conversation completely – said *"Look, I don't want to be pushy but I'm going to need to get back to the conference centre. Say, I have a great idea. I expect you've got the odd late party invite but why don't we get together for dinner tonight, on me of course. It beats the hell out of trying to survive on all that finger buffet stuff they serve everywhere. And – I'll be honest – I've promised to give my fixer a meal tonight. She's good company but it would be great to have a new face. And she knows this place inside out if you need any tips. Shall we say the restaurant at Hotel du Ville at 8? You'll be on the doorstep of your own hotel and you can go on elsewhere when you need."*

Fox realised that he was indeed hungry. He had been subsisting on hors d'oeuvre trays for 2 days. *"Sounds great"* he said. *"I'll look forward to it."*

4

The restaurant, as seemed to be the case everywhere there, oozed 'smooth'. As Fox was led to the table, he noted that first there was plenty of room between tables (no doubt to facilitate privacy); but second that people at the tables that were occupied had no interest in him or his doings. Later, they touched on that; and Brightwell noted with a laugh *"Well it goes with the territory. If you think you're the main guy, you're not interested in who's around you unless it's Donald Trump walking past. For us in private equity, that's really a bonus, being able to move around without too much 'traffic noise'."*

Brightwell was sitting there waiting, as a good host, and rose to introduce his companion. *"Hi, Marcus. Great you could come. This is Caroline McEwan."* An immaculately dressed woman in her late 30s, Marcus guessed, rose and shook his hand. *"Hello. I don't do Americanisms unless I'm with Liford people only. I'm British, so hello."* She was wearing a well-cut but quite tight short black evening dress, which Marcus couldn't help noticing showed off a fine trim figure.

The hosts ordered Martinis. Marcus decided to venture no further than G&T. The evening progressed rapidly and well. Brightwell was attentive to Caroline but adept at ensuring that Marcus quickly felt that he, not Caroline, was the main guest. Caroline ran through a few funny stories about things she had seen or 'urban myths' that ran with the WEF story. This, it turned out, was her fifth year; and, unlike Fox, who had just had access to part of a couple of days of a London-based fixer, it was obvious that Caroline was all-Liford and had been for some years. *"Liford gets all my attention"* she said at one point. *"Or, rather Bernie – our President and CEO does. People like Frank here are happy to share."*

There was very little business talk until Fox had downed an excellent fillet steak and about half a bottle of good French red. He felt a lot better for it. And when Brightwell skilfully brought the subject round to Fox's life and frustrations as the WH CEO, he found it easy to talk, indeed quite hard not to ramble on. Brightwell and Caroline both listened intently and, as months later Fox replayed that evening, he realised how clever they had been in getting him to open up about the challenges facing him and WH.

Towards the end of a couple of hours that he had enjoyed more than anything in the week, Brightwell brought the evening expertly to an end. "We mustn't monopolise you, Marcus. I'm sure you've got several late parties to attend. I'll settle this up and we'll walk you back to your hotel. They supply snow grips here for your shoes and, if we three link arms I'm sure we can manage the hundred yards or so. If I may, I'll think about some of the problems you have. They are not entirely unfamiliar. We own stakes in a couple of Lloyds insurance syndicates and we've provided quite a lot of the financing that got Care Homes Inc. out of its last administration. Give me a few weeks and perhaps we can repeat this enjoyable meal somewhere on our home ground in Mayfair. *"I shall insist on coming"* said Caroline. *"Liford don't feed me nearly as well as they should."*

Fox was not seriously the worse for drink. But nevertheless, he made sure he clung to Caroline and Brightwell as they introduced him to snow grips and, taking a firm grip one on either side, got him back to his hotel. Ten seconds after he had shut his room door behind him, Fox knew he had no intention of trogging off to the couple of parties on his list for that evening. Hell, he was the CEO. He was going to go with the flow.

5

Fox returned quickly to normality when, at the end of the week, he swapped the snow of Switzerland for the rain of Manchester. In addition to the work that had accumulated while he had been away, there was a good deal of follow up by email or letter necessary on people and firms he had met. He did note, with pleasure, a short message from Brightwell promising to be in touch; and then, with the pressure of work, he thought no more about it.

Brightwell did not in fact get in touch for about 6 weeks. But then came a quite chatty email from him, suggesting that Fox find time for a dinner with Brightwell next time he – Fox – was in London. *"I know WH are H.Q'd in Manchester but I'm sure you must get down to London quite often"* wrote Brightwell. *"Just let me know when it's convenient and Caroline will fix something up."*

Fox was, in fact, typically spending one day a week in London at that point, trying to push ahead with plans for that big deal, with the aid (he sometimes thought 'over the body of') his financial advisers. So, it was less than 3 weeks later that Fox found himself sharing his woes with Brightwell and McEwan one evening in what (his Google check had shown) was one of the best restaurants in Mayfair. Fox finished what had been a 10 minute monologue on the sloth and lack of vision of his City advisers in finding the deal he needed and sat back, still nursing the end of his first G&T of the evening.

Brightwell chuckled. *"Doesn't sound like much fun. And you mean WH doesn't even have its own office in the City? You have to rely on your advisers for office space here and secretarial help?"* Brightwell exchanged a brief smile with Caroline. *"Well, of course, they think they've got you where they want you – dependent on them. Let's show them a different side to you. Our Mayfair offices have plenty of room for you, Caroline can fix you up with temporary secretarial support. All easy, needn't cost you a penny – it won't cost us. Next time you see your advisers just tell them you are moving in with Liford Holdings and watch their faces. They'll wet themselves thinking you may be deserting them. I'll bet you see a marked improvement in their treatment of you within days."*

"That's very kind of you" replied Fox *"but I couldn't possibly impose like that."* *"Nonsense"* Caroline cut in. *"It'll be really easy – we can have it up and running by this time next week. Do say 'yes'; I haven't got much going on at present; it'll help to keep me out of mischief."* She smiled at him as she said it; she really was pretty.

This was how, just 6 days later, Fox found himself sitting in what he could only call a luxury office – certainly by comparison with anything WH had – about 150 yards from the restaurant of the previous week. He shut his eyes and breathed in deeply. He had never smelt leather of such opulence; he had never before had an office desk of such size. The secretary provided seemed several cuts in education and demeanour *above* Mrs Hastings back in Manchester. Wonderful on every count; and, to top it off, his City advisers were – as Brightwell had predicted – already sounding more supportive.

"There is just one thing" said Brightwell as he looked in *"Your own secretary and your Advisers will know you are here. Best to make no secret of it. But do make sure they are clear what this is and isn't. You are not here to work on a deal that affects WH; there is nothing going on that will affect your share price or needs disclosing under Stock Exchange rules. People tend to paint firms like Liford in the blackest colours. You are here because we met up at the WEF and WH doesn't have anything of its own – fit for a CEO anyway – in London; end of story."*

The new arrangements continued happily, as they had begun. About 3 weeks in, Fox took Caroline out for dinner to say thank you for what she had done for him. This, in turn, that evening led him to discover that her flat was near that plush restaurant, that she made good coffee… and that she had an even better figure out of the little black evening dress than in it. He hadn't intended that last discovery but, the next morning, he couldn't honestly regret having made it. She had been very sweet. Fox had felt very much at home.

6

Fox began a routine where he would spend each Wednesday in London. Tuesday night would be at his hotel, Wednesday night in Caroline's flat. His wife did insist on coming with him to London once but, so far as Fox could see, he might reasonably hope the arrangement would last for months; and he certainly felt better for it.

The first sign that there might be more to think about was when Brightwell dropped into Fox's borrowed office in Mayfair one Wednesday morning. Brightwell perched himself on the edge of the desk. *"Look, we've been contemplating your problems at WH. We think Liford can help in several ways. It's not just our direct holdings in your area of business. Our insurance interests at Lloyds for example barely rate in size against WH's insurance. But we have lots of capital for the right deals; and we have a lot of 'friends' – people who have their own commercial interests AND who are willing to put money into investments we suggest.*

What we don't have is enough of an idea about WH's other activities, the care homes and what you hope to get out of them. We'd also like to understand your insurance business better. What I suggest is that we open a due diligence room in your Manchester HQ and start running the slide rule over your business. No commitment on either side of course though, if you want a bit of a boost to your share price, you could put out a short Stock Exchange notice saying what Liford are doing. We don't have shares on publicly quoted exchanges so there is really nothing for us to announce. Our CFO Hitesh can bring a small team up to Manchester – shouldn't take more than 2 or 3 weeks. And I'll make sure Caroline comes up occasionally too; she tells me you and she get along just fine, which is great."

After a brief consultation with what Fox still insisted on calling his 'financial advisers', a brief Stock Exchange note was duly issued on behalf of WH; and within 10 days, Hitesh (who turned out to a frighteningly bright Harvard-trained man) and a small team were installed in Manchester. Several good things followed. As Brightwell had predicted, the WH share price ticked up; and several of the weightier dailies even ran background articles on WH, something of a rarity in recent years. One even featured a carefully choreographed interview with Fox himself.

Fox's City advisers had indeed taken umbrage at Liford's involvement. One of them – whom Fox had known for years – had gone to the length of warning Fox to be very careful. *"You should sup with those devils at*

Liford with a very long spoon and preferably not at all." But, boy, his advisers were clearly now moving a lot faster at WH's urging. Even one or two of Fox's assistants back in Manchester began treating him with a new deference. It didn't take more than 10 minutes on Google to establish that, wherever Liford had been involved in corporate restructuring, a good deal of human and corporate blood had been spilled on the way to what, so far, had generally been large profits for Liford and their fellow investors. So, perhaps some of his Manchester colleagues were starting to think about their longer-term interests.

The one less satisfactory point was that Caroline's visits to Manchester were – had to be – innocuous. Fox realised only too well that, while a Mayfair-based tryst was fairly easy to set up, there were far too many prying eyes in his home base for him to risk anything with Caroline there. Fortunately, Hitesh and his team proved little problem. Yes, they asked a lot of questions but they were not afraid to get their hands dirty with the figures and they seemed to work extraordinary hours. Even when they asked to be able to visit a random set of WH properties, they kept the demands on WH to a minimum.

7

Fox's pleasant little world became markedly more complex another 4 weeks later. He had managed to get away to London, on the basis of needing to attend an open meeting with potential investors and he had spent Tuesday night in his hotel. He knew enough of how his City advisers worked to be able to reckon that the meeting, scheduled for 11 a.m. would segue into a pleasant lunch at the firm's excellent dining facilities around 1.15. He had provisionally arranged to meet Caroline at 6 and was looking forward to a very relaxed evening in her flat.

The day started well enough but he made the mistake of popping back to Liford's offices about 4 p.m., after what indeed had been an excellent lunch, to drop off some papers; and Brightwell appeared in Fox's office within a minute of Fox's own arrival. *"I've been meaning to have a word"* said Brightwell, taking up his usual position seated on the corner of Fox's desk. *"We've got a package together that we think you might be interested in. Delay going back to Manchester tomorrow morning and we'll take you through it. But just a taster for you for now; we've found some investors with capital and assets that will be of use. The aim will be to create a new WH, oozing with capital, new ideas and a hugely bright future. More tomorrow."* And, with that, Brightwell left Fox to his thoughts.

Later, over a drink, Caroline seemed unable to throw more light on what was being planned. *"Don't be boring, darling"* she said, wriggling out of his embrace as he asked her, for a third time, what she knew about this latest development. *"This is all above my paygrade. Let's just enjoy ourselves tonight. You can bet, whatever it is, that Brighty will have your interests second only to Liford's in whatever he has got planned."*

Fox was too worried to enjoy himself as much as he'd hoped. He then slept badly and, by 10 a.m. the next morning – after just a cup of coffee with Caroline – Fox was pacing the Liford Board room (which was considerably more opulent than his borrowed office and full of what looked like high-tech gadgets and screens.) Brightwell breezed in with Hitesh and a couple of his team at 10 sharp and got down to business.

"You know what you guys at WH need. You've got a top 3 rating in several parts of the UK insurance market. But the UK is played out – too much regulation, too much competition. You need a big European or American insurer in the group to give you new worlds to conquer, especially in Asia where there is a sea of

new business waiting to be tapped. You also need money, because growth of the kind you need in those new markets needs a lot of money behind it. And you're not a Tesla or We Works who can blind people with optimistic forecasts of taking over the world AND get them to put money in up front to finance you. So you need to raise money on your own.

Now, you can raise some of that cash with a rights issue but there is a strict limit to what that will bring in. Much better to do two other things as well. First, find a couple of big (but not too big) foreign companies in your line of business and take them over, using your shares so the cash stays intact. That's like being on steroids, bulks you up and makes the market talk of vast global expansion plans, being able to set global prices and so on… much more what you need. Second, cash in the rest of your portfolio, the Care Homes and the rest, at a great price, well above the limited sum you've got them marked down at present in the books, so that – with the rights issue – you do have some serious money with which to expand.

Put it another way. You take the current WH pizza, which is a mixture of pepperoni (health and other insurance) and boring old mixed vegetables (care homes). You rearrange the kitchen and bring some guys with foreign pepperoni (insurance abroad) and produce a huge new pepperoni pizza baked by WH and containing only healthy profitable world-wide insurance. You also flip the existing WH care home/retirement village pizza back into a larger mixing bowl, sell your homes at a great price and walk away from the boring unsexy part of the business – providing day to day care for grumpy old folk.

Your current shareholders see the chance, with their existing shares and the rights issue, of buying into the new story on the cheap. Your foreign insurers see the chance of joining the big global league by merging with you; sure they lose their independence but what's so great about being a small fish in a large pond, if you can be part of a global giant? And the care home people you sell to also get what they desperately need – which is to bulk up on the steroids of your homes, putting them together with what they've got."

None of this was really new to Fox. Over the weeks, his City advisers had said some of the same things. But Brightwell had put it all together – an enticing 'big picture'. And, maybe, Liford had the key missing bits of the jigsaw ready to hand. That was what made the difference. Over the next hour, Hitesh followed up with what seemed an endless PowerPoint presentation, with screens around the Board room popping into action as if they truly had a life of their own. The gist of the presentation was unremittingly positive. Take 2 (WH's insurance), add 1 (an Italian insurer he had never heard of); add another (a mid-West US general insurer he had heard of before) and Hitesh could arrive at a total of 5 – followed later in the presentation by 6 and, finally, 7.

Brightwell listened to the presentation and at the end summarised. *"I talked about making new and bigger pizzas. The secret of all Merger & Acquisition work of the kind we do at Liford is just that. Provide the ingredients to make those bigger pizzas. Show pictures of just how good those pizzas are going to be. Make sure each pizza has only things in it which turn the viewer on, so the investor who likes pepperoni only sees what he likes. And leave them to imagine the future for themselves. If we talk about WH's earnings per share rising by 40% in 5 years and if we do a decent job of it, you can bet half of them, in their mind, will have a picture where actually it could be 80. You encourage the frothier analysts to write about their 80% vision – and, lo and behold, you've set up the conditions for it all actually to happen."*

"I have to admit that all sounds impressive. First, though, tell me what Liford get out of this" commented Fox. *"Well, I don't want to give away too many trade secrets"* replied Brightwell. *"But we might have some existing interest in one or both of those insurance companies. We certainly have interests in Care Homes in the UK from what we picked up after the last big crash in that sector. And our whole business model for outside investors is based on the fact that we bring them a steady flow of exciting new investment opportunities and get them in on the ground floor. This package fits that model perfectly.*

Now, we need to proceed quickly and carefully" Bright went on. *"I can give you today to contact your Chairman and any absolutely other key people you want to keep on-side with. You'll need to say very little because, after all as far as the world is concerned, you don't know anything of the detail at all. Tomorrow at 7a.m. we'll get a Notice out through the Stock Exchange to say that Liford will be putting a proposition to WH that will significantly affect your firm's shares. You get your Chairman to organise a Board meeting in the next few days, to 'consider their position'. You will need to make sure that this 'position' involves WH opening talks with us. Your share price will start to pick up. And you can placate your City advisers by getting them in to handle WH's side of the negotiations with us."*

"God" said Fox. *"Slow down. I can think of dozens of questions that line of action will raise, answers I will have to have. And suppose I look at all this, we the WH Board do, and have issues? I can't just stand up, seemingly out of nothing, and commit WH to a huge change of course just like that, especially without knowing about and having crawled over the detailed numbers."*

Brightwell leered at Fox – it was the only word Fox could find afterwards to describe it. *"I think you'll find a way, old boy. If you're not sure, I suggest you get Caroline to show you some of the photos that your wife and your Board will be seeing of your recent London night-time wanderings if you don't bring your Board with you. Those pictures are certainly pretty lively. I didn't think you had it in you but Caroline tells me you very definitely do. And the piccies certainly support that.*

Now, I'll leave you with Hitesh. He can answer any immediate practical questions you have and maybe help you rehearse your immediate pitch to the Chairman. The thing to do is to get your Chairman as excited as we are about the possibilities. He is currently Chair of a third-rate company going nowhere; within 6-9 months he can be Chair of a hugely bigger company with real prospects. You can all pay yourselves large bonuses for having had the wit to organise it, even if we have done most of the work. And then you can pay yourselves a lot more going forward for having to run such a big company. I have a burner mobile here for you" – Brightwell produced a small package and handed it over to Fox. *"That is what you use to contact me for any serious discussions over the next few months. It can't be traced to me and, in the package, you'll find a couple of numbers you can get me on with that phone, which equally aren't traceable to me. Anything that the regulators shouldn't know about – that's what you use the phone for.*

Finally, I do suggest you think calmly about all this before you see Caroline tonight. She was just doing what we pay her to do and, if it's any consolation, I know she has enjoyed her time with you much more than she expected to. Provided you're careful, I'm sure she'll let you go on seeing her while all the Stock Market stuff gets ironed out. I do think, though, that you ought to start planning a very big present for her, for when your post-merger company pay-off comes through."

With that, Brightwell rose and left, leaving Hitesh (who had heard all this) clearly wondering where and how he should now begin. Eventually, Hitesh just lent across to Fox and said *"I'll leave you to gather your thoughts for a few minutes. Then we can talk if you want."*

It took Fox 30 minutes to calm down and another 30 to think rationally about his position. With what Brightwell had said, some things fell into position with a sickening thud. No wonder Caroline had been comfortable with him staying in her flat. The story also explained why she had been so keen to throw the bedclothes away in their love-making. *"Giving me room to move"* as she had put it at the time.

On the other hand, the more he thought about the rest of it the better that all looked too. The proposition Liford was putting together certainly had its plus points, not least that owning an Italian insurer would give them a safe base in the EU however Brexit turned out. Fox also knew he had to have a deal and, when he examined his conscience, he had to admit that he must really have expected Liford to come up with something. It was just so quick and there was the sickener of God knows what photos that were around. He would have to get a guarantee somehow that they would be destroyed if he delivered on his side of the bargain. And, as for Caroline, well he had enjoyed himself; and, now he knew she was just a high-class call girl, he would treat her like that. If she was going to get 'a big present' from him, she could earn it.

With that, Fox called Hitesh back in and said that he, Fox, had enough to be going on with. He then sent a curt email to Caroline saying he'd see her in due course (he was sure Brightwell would have told her what Fox now knew). He then went back to his hotel and got blind drunk. The Chairman could wait.

8

Notices affecting listed companies on the Stock Exchange in the UK typically come out at 7 a.m., well before the market opens at 8. The following morning, Thursday, and despite a raging hangover, Fox had the presence – once he had checked that the Notice had gone out – to ring his Chairman before he had heard the news elsewhere. Liford had provided enough detail in their Notice – including the names of the possible insurers who might come in – that Fox could talk a little about what seemed to be planned, without giving away any hint that he must have had prior notice himself. With the Chairman, and then with other Board members, Fox was resolutely upbeat. Typically, he would say in conclusion *"Obviously, we haven't got much idea of what this might mean in practice. Or whether it's likely to come off. But [illegible] re worth a great [illegible] t looks as though [illegible] need. I'm down [illegible] d and to our City [illegible] soonest, to decide [illegible] re to get our teeth [illegible]*

[illegible] ace in Manchester [illegible] a time or a place [illegible] d Board members. [illegible], Fox had worked [illegible] back-door link to [illegible] eck what his, Fox's, strategy [illegible]

Thanks largely to that, [illegible] d had little difficulty in agreeing that two work teams should be set up in WH to investigate the named Italian and US insurers. A third Working Party should look at proposals for the care homes; and Fox ensured that he personally would be sitting at the centre of all this work to be certain it drove forward in ways he could live with. The final thing agreed was a short press statement, saying in essence that WH was in the mood to expand but that WH and no-one else would be deciding what was good for the company. By the Stock Exchange close on Friday (before the Press Statement had come out), WH's share price had risen by about 4%.

Fox then found himself spending most of Saturday giving 'off the record' press briefings to the better quality Sunday and Weekly Daily papers. One of the Sundays managed a supposedly in-depth column that weekend.

But most of the material hit the world the following week. By then, apart from wishing each day could be 20% longer, Fox felt he was in a pretty good place. His periodic telephone chats with Brightwell were going well. He had even patched up a truce with Caroline, though so far that had only been done by phone, not face-to-face. And the outside business world was starting to talk about a 'sleeping giant (WH) being on the move' under a dynamic new (hardly accurate but who cared) CEO. There was a lot for Fox to feel good about.

9

Over the next 8 weeks a lot of paddling was done under the water but, to the untrained eye, it didn't look as though any of the ducks had moved very far. One WH Working Party had descended on the Italian insurer and, after a pleasant few days in Rome, reported back favourably. The existing Italian business was broadly similar to that of WH but its operations were years behind its British counterpart; and, in the Italian firm, there was clearly a forward-looking group of employees who could see real value in their being taken over by WH. Likewise, the Working Party that reported back from Nevada was generally complementary about the US target, though here the proviso was that the American political scene about health insurance was incredibly confused. So what the options for WH there would actually be were difficult to forecast. But there was a real and generally profitable business out there already, so – provided WH didn't pay too much – that deal looked viable too.

The biggest concern was over the last leg of what became generally known round WH as 'the Liford package', which was the proposed sale of the several hundred WH care homes and retirement villages to a firm that had emerged about 5 years earlier from the last big upheaval in that industry. The trouble here was that this firm, owned wholly by a US private equity firm that never took prisoners (and which seemingly had close connections with Liford), was widely regarded – not least around the press – as 'toxic'.

Much of what had happened 5 years earlier had been the fault of a quite different firm. This had built a little empire of care homes and had then borrowed heavily on the real estate involved and paid itself huge dividends up front with the money. The large and expensive debt then had to be financed out of current income; and this was roughly at the same time as care home costs started to soar and local authorities became ever less willing to foot the resultant bills. In the end, around the middle of the decade, a new owner arrived, buying out the old business for £1 and reneging on much of the existing debt. At the time, there had been alarmist talk about thousands of elderly residents being turfed out onto the street. Also, there was lots of press comment on how owners – particularly private equity – shouldn't be allowed to own businesses that were cash cows (because of the reasonably safe projected flows of resident fees), when there wasn't really anyone to guard their residents' interests.

This debate had new life breathed into it by the Liford proposal. WH would – in the majority press view – be cashing in on its homes and walking away from the problem, leaving the residents at the mercy of the new US owners.

Fox and his Chairman talked this over one evening in Manchester. *"I've talked to our PR people"* said Fox *"and, of course, it's much less black and white than the press like to make out. WH isn't entirely walking away. We shall want to have agreements in place with the new owner because – in about 40% of our homes – we have clinic or dementia ward beds. We shall want to keep those. It would be a pretty strange insurer that didn't have any beds to back its health insurance. So we will have continuing links in respect of that and can exercise some oversight on what Liford and this related firm get up to. And, of course, most of the elderly who have bought packages in our retirement villages have leases which set out a lot of what can and can't be done by any new owner. So, there is a limit to what Liford can do there. But I can see that these leaseholders have no reason to welcome the change.*

The trouble for us is that these homes are in our books for a song – mostly reflecting the property prices they were fetching when we bought them. Liford think the new owners will pay up to three times book value, based on current property prices. Whatever the gap, we can credit that straight to our insurance reserves, making it hugely much easier for us to grow our new business with the regulators' blessing – here or abroad. It's a key part of the deal. We can't do without it."

The Chairman swilled his whisky thoughtfully in the glass. *"Any ideas?"* he asked. Fox gave a snort. *"There isn't much need to do anything about the Care Homes serving Local Authorities. The best we've come up with so far is that the new owners promise to leave current fees unchanged for at least 2 years. But that would be like a crocodile promising not to eat anything just yet. The trickier part is the wealthier leaseholders in our Retirement Villages. There is a half-baked idea that we should offer shares in WH to all these care home lease holders, whether they are shareholders now or not. But £1,000-worth of shares a head for every leaseholder probably means a bill of at least* £10 *million. And, frankly, £1,000 is not going to sway anyone. I think we're just going to have to tough it out. There aren't that many of them and they've got some protection anyway from their leases."*

10

As it happened, the same subject was being discussed at just that time, in one of WH's Retirement Villages. It wasn't typical in many ways, not least because it was unusually large (well over 100 apartments) and virtually brand-new. It was also wholly private sector – housing people who were elderly (over 70) and who paid for everything themselves. In other respects, it was not so different from the normal WH Care Home– not least because it had a clinical and dementia floor run totally by WH.

The newly elected Chair of the Resident Association – John Deedes – looked thoughtfully into his beer, sitting in the new and largely deserted bar area with Graham Ingham, one of the 2 people on the new Association Committee with whom he was always happy to spend time. It was around 8 p.m. and, with the average resident aged around 80, there weren't too many other people around. *"Bit of a bummer walking into this problem in our first 6 months here"* he said. *"I suppose there must be a good chance that the deal will break down, in whole or part. But, as you suggested, Graham, I've read through what it says in our leases and I can't see much help there. These leases have, of course, been drawn up by WH lawyers and, as you'd expect they tend to be very vague on our rights and WH's obligations and very specific on our obligations and WH rights.*

It looks as though, subject to a simple court procedure, WH can pass their involvement in the leases onto a third party without our agreement. I think we can assume that the same WH lawyers who drafted the lease will have no trouble fitting current circumstances into something that will be immune from legal challenge. I think our choices are quite simple. We either quietly go along with it – and the thousands of other residents on other WH homes will be in the same boat. Or we fight it on the only basis that might work – political agitation by Middle England against evil private equity capitalism."

Graham smiled slightly at the idea that the residents of the home might be up to agitation on anything other than the quality of the food or the cleaning arrangements. These were the subjects which covered 80% of his normal intercourse with residents as a member of the Residents' Association; and he couldn't readily see a mass uprising over the possibility of a private equity owner, no matter how dubious its reputation. *"Yes"* he said. *"I've been thinking along those lines but slightly more broadly. Let's get another pint apiece before the barman goes home – he usually gives up about 8.30 because everyone has gone back to their rooms. And I'll explain what I have in mind."*

About 10 minutes later – nothing much moved quickly in the home – Graham settled himself comfortably and resumed. *"it's a bit of a roundabout story. But it begins with my family, as most things have done in my life. You know what we do – you're drinking a pint of our best ale now. And, as you know, the Ingham's Brewery is both a pillar of the local industry round here and still largely family-owned.*

Not just because it's good PR, the family has always believed in putting long-serving staff near the front of the queue when it comes to sharing out the profits. We've never had a day's strike. Many of our employees have never worked with anyone else but Ingham's. And so far we've avoided the worst problems the beer industry has had to face in recent years. I thank my lucky stars every night that we went for new specialist ales right when they first became trendy, about 20 years ago. In short, thanks largely to that, we're solvent, we have cash in the bank and not too many rivals breathing down our necks.

"Now, one of the bits of the jigsaw I've long had in mind remains the fact that we have nothing or perhaps I should say nowhere to send our retired staff when they're getting on. As you may know, Ingham's has an active charity which gets 5% of total profits each year to use. And, years ago, I raised with the Charity Commission the possibility that we might want to buy and run some sort of Retirement or Care Home for our staff as they retired. Now, the Commission never say 'yes' outright to any idea passed across them if it's not bolted down. But, at the time, I got a cautious OK in principle from them and I had some changes made to the Charity's Memorandum, making clear that

owning and running something like that for ex-staff would be within the things the Charity could do.

Nothing more has ever come of it. If you bought the land there is here in this Village and built on it, you'd be looking at spending at least £30 million, maybe a lot more. So, Ingham's have never done anything to make the idea a reality. But, when I heard about this WH move, I couldn't help but wonder. The apartments here have largely sold, so the value of what is left plus the reversionary rights at the end of the 120 year leases would be worth only a tiny fraction of what it cost to build the place – WH got the building money back when they sold the leases. And the fact that there are only a few vacancies here now is just what we want. Only a few long-standing Ingham's staff retire each year and most of them will, initially be able to look after themselves. If the Charity owned this place, we'd be sure to get a few vacancies more each year, as leaseholders here die and their executors sell on. And we could take in people who were still hale and hearty and those who already need medical care. The executors would be free to sell to whom they like but the Charity could make sure it was offering top dollar if it wanted the lease for an Ingham's retiree. Indeed, it almost looks as though our leases were drawn up to facilitate that. The owners of the freehold here have to be offered an empty flat before it is put on the market. Just what we would want.

Think about it. I have and I think it's brilliant. Just one problem. How do we get WH or Liford to notice us in the general stampede and take time out to negotiate a deal with us when they're trying to deal with several hundred newly acquired Care Homes? That's the bit I can't fathom."

With that, John and Graham finished off their drinks and made it back to their rooms. That night, Deedes felt better than he had for some time. Here, in Ingham's Charity was an institution with the money to back this place. Surely, there must be a way to get WH and/or Liford to look in their direction.

11

An idea as to how WH or Liford might be forced to give attention to one home out of many came first from Victoria Morse, the third member of the Residents' Association Committee with whom Deedes felt at home. Deedes had checked first with Ingham that it was OK to widen the circle by one and then, over coffee in the Residents' Lounge had unveiled the idea to Victoria. The way he put it, the question was really two-fold. First, would residents be comfortable with Ingham's Charity taking over the Home? What sort of protections might they seek in that case? Second, how to engage with WH or Liford?

Victoria had had a significant executive career during her working years. She was already au fait with the WH/ Liford scheme and readily took on board why Ingham's

Charity might want to take on the home. When Deedes had finished, he sat back and waited; Victoria would comment when she was ready.

"Interesting" she finally said. *"Personally, I don't see any problem with selling here the idea of Ingham's as an owner. Thoughtful people here might want some assurance that, if the Brewery were taken over, the nature of the Charity's purpose wasn't changed to their detriment. But that should be easy enough to fix. It should be a 'no-brainer' that Ingham's would be a better owner than Liford; and I don't think people are too wild about WH either. And, even at their age, most of the Residents here will be too PC to air what might be their real concern – which is that Ingham's flood the place with 'unsuitable' residents. The fact is, I know people here are already starting to worry about how their families will be able to on-sell when the time comes. People know that, despite a huge sales effort, WH haven't managed to sell all the apartments here, even first time round. Also, if they think about it, people will realise that they won't be around long enough to see any significant changes to who is here. We're all elderly, some of us are sick and most of us – if we're wise – don't have a time horizon of more than a few years. No problems there I think. But it would help – leaseholders know and like Graham – if he could be installed as a key Adviser or something to The Charity while he's alive. That would give a 'face' for the Charity that people can relate to. You and I could have some 'safeguarding' role if we want.*

The second question is much more difficult but I think I can see a way. Did you know that Mrs Whyte in Number 70 is actually the mother of our local MP? No reason why you should, as she doesn't share his surname, she remarried late in life. I've known her for years and Martin, the MP, is very much a mother's boy. I'm sure he'll want to help if his mother asks him. And, as he's currently a Minister in the Competition Authority, my guess is that he'll either have a role to play in clearing the competition side of the WH deal or will be able to influence those who do. If, for example, WH thought that a one-off deal for our little home was the price for getting the whole shebang agreed, I suspect that would be pretty easy to arrange."

Deedes sat back in amazement. Brilliant. And, on the spot, he agreed – before taking it back to Graham – that Victoria should start to 'warm' Mrs Whyte up to talk in due course to her son.

12

Complex corporate restructurings can take a long and, more importantly, an uncertain length of time. WH had to convince their insurance regulators that it would be safe to buy the Italian and American businesses. Those businesses had to convince their own regulators that the British acquirer was a 'safe' new owner, which – in the Italian case – also meant sweeping over some remaining bad Brexit feeling. Liford and WH together had to convince the UK Competition Authority that the Care Home tie-up should be passed. WH had to keep up the positive flow of speculation about the future that would underpin a share rights issue for them. And Liford had to get their ducks or (as Brightwell once put it) their golden geese lined up to provide the capital necessary to buy the WH homes.

For Deedes and his colleagues, the job was simpler in one respect; they just had to persuade leaseholders not to object if Ingham's Charity did buy the site from WH. And Victoria proved a very effective communicator with her fellow leaseholders. As she put it after one of the 4 lengthy meetings that were held for leaseholders *"We're nearly there. We shall have to get the Charity to show willing on a couple of possible innovations. A lot of leaseholders, for example, want a little shop on the site to save them going into town. But, as long as we keep those aspirations down to a sensible level, that will be fine. What we do have some work to do on, though, is to convince leaseholders that the key WH staff will 'come over' and stay with us; and we have to show that the Charity, with our involvement early on, knows enough to keep the Village functioning. We also need to be able to promise them that WH will keep running the clinic and dementia floor.*

One or two bright sparks wanted to go further and have us leaseholders buy up the site. But I explained that would cost them a fortune in putting up the capital for the purchase price and that outsiders (not least our bank) would want to know that something substantial like the Charity is standing behind the Village."

Perhaps the stickiest point in the discussions came over what the Village might be called in the new world. The Charity originally rooted for 'The Brewer's Alms' but residents dismissed this as sounding like a pub and not a very up-market one at that. Thanks again to Victoria, a compromise was finally reached on 'The Four Winds'. *"I was thinking of Mahjong when I came up with that, plus the fact that it is pretty windy as well as wet round here. Several of our more religious members liked the name because there is something in the Bible about the four winds, though I forget where. More importantly, it sounds pretty neutral; and I've convinced Graham that, if his lot still want The Brewer's Alms in ten years, it would be more appropriate than it is now, because by then it will be mostly Ingham's people here. So, unless anyone can think of a problem we haven't identified, I suggest we go for a new company called The Four Winds. It will be 100% owned by the Charity and, at least to start with the Directors will be 4 from the Charity plus the 3 of us to help with continuity."*

Deedes found his role now lay mainly with the finances. Graham had at least as relevant a background as he did; but Graham could hardly be classed as independent, given his life-long involvement with the brewer.

Much of that financial work revolved around two things. How much could The Four Winds (i.e. the Charity) be expected to pay WH or Liford for the Village? And how would the finances develop once the WH layers of protection fell away?

13

This strand of work came together most obviously, Deedes recalled afterwards, in a daylong meeting with the bank (fortunately the same bank for the Village as the one used by the Charity) and the Charity Trustees who would have to sign off on the deal as being fair value for the Charity.

Deedes had made a lengthy presentation. *"I'll start right at the beginning and take you through how WH must view this Village and, therefore, what they think a reasonable price might be. I have assumed we're buying from WH not Liford. Because WH are the owners now, they are likely to be more 'reasonable' than Liford; and we definitely want WH to keep control of the clinic and dementia ward, so it makes sense to negotiate with them. Finally, if we assumed WH sell to Liford and then we buy from them, there would be 2 sets of legal fees and stamp duty rather than one, which is in nobody's interests.*

Now, there are several sets of income that WH might expect if they retain ownership. First, ***ground rents****. Each year, each of the leaseholders in the Village has to pay a sum – currently £250 a year and linked to future inflation – in Ground Rent to WH. Fortunately, as far I can establish, WH hasn't done what some freeholders do and on-sold those rights to an insurance company or pension fund. Existing leaseholders here know about this future charge and don't have any grounds for disputing it. I suggest the Charity leaves things as they are, so Ground Rents in future flow to it, as the new Freeholder.*

Now, a few of you may know that there was some discussion before the last Election as to whether Ground Rents should be abolished. Personally, I don't think that will happen and, if it did, it's interesting that people who favoured its abolition often exempted 'small' annual charges like our £250. So it's likely to continue. So, I think we just have to bite the bullet and pay WH upfront in compensation for the ground rents. The Charity will, over time, get quite a lot of this back, as non-Ingham's leaseholders continue to pay ground rent.

Second, ***sales and transaction fees.*** *WH still have 8 apartments to sell. This is despite a huge sales effort over many months. Now, the Charity will want these vacant apartments, to house the first wave of Ingham's retirees and I would have thought WH would be keen to get cash for them. The total price for the 8 apartments is £2.4 million according to the Village web-site. My guess is they'd settle for £1.6-£1.7 million to get shot of them all in one go. The next part is more tricky. Existing leaseholders have to pay 10% to WH when they on-sell their apartment, which is usually* *because of death. 100 apartments, maybe 12 deaths/departures a year, so very roughly 10% of apartments turning over each year, maybe £3.5 million a year in total, making about £350,000 a year to the owners of the freehold. The people I've consulted suggest that maybe 7 years' worth of commission money up front, say* £2.6 *million might make WH feel they were being adequately compensated for losing future flows, especially as it gives them cash in hand and gets them out of the messy and expensive business of overseeing the sales. It also gets them out of the risk that sales of these things go on being difficult, or that the market gets even worse.*

Finally, in this area, the freeholders get the leases revert to them at the end of the lease. We are talking about 119 years time. I suggest we start from – and stick with – the basis that these rights are effectively worthless as of now. WH are concerned about next year, not 2140.

Then, we have ***clinical/nursing fees.*** *This needn't be an issue. We know that WH want to continue to run their clinics and dementia wards –they see that as part of their on-going insurance provision. And it's good for us too. Existing leaseholders bought on the expectation that these services would be available on site. They will be – and this is the area of the business where the Charity would have struggled most to step into WH's shoes. So the status quo costs us nothing and should suit everyone.*

Finally, but we can't quantify this, we think WH charge some of their central services, like legal and accounting, to each of their care homes. But we know from the accounts of other WH Villages like ours that most of the money WH spends reflects local services; and those costs get paid for by the local residents by way of a service charge. Reception services, motor vehicles, gardening, things like that. WH stop being responsible for these services if they sell to us. We take them on; WH costs and income go down by an equal amount. Our lease holders go on paying their service charges but to the Charity, not WH. Maybe WH have to let a central lawyer or accountant go but there should be no significant costs for WH, given they are facing a much bigger upheaval than just parting with one home.

In short, if you add it all up, my guess is that WH would eventually settle for about £6.5 million for this Village and bite your hand off if you offer £7.5 million. Those are certainly the numbers I have rehearsed with Ingham's and – the Trustees present here will, I hope confirm – they seem to find that quite doable. If I may say, they also understand that, over the years ahead, they will be paying considerably more as they buy the leases up. But they also realise this is a golden chance to buy up a newly and purpose-built Village that cost tens of millions to build and which is in an area in which their intended beneficiaries mostly live and feel comfortable with. And without the huge upfront cost if they started from scratch. All we have to do now, if you agree, is get WH to see it the same way."

14

Deedes and his two colleagues readily agreed that it made sense to approach WH not Liford. They also agreed that a preliminary call on the Minister would make sense, as Victoria was able to confirm that Mrs Whyte had made her views very clearly known to her son. They went, as a threesome, to one of the MP's constituency sessions, which were always held on a Friday. They were third in a small queue and had to wait only about 20 minutes. While he waited, Deedes looked around to see if he could see any particular security measures but the Minister either felt that these were unnecessary or had them well hidden.

None of the three had met the Minister before and, after introductions, Victoria kicked off. *"Minister, I'm sure you are a busy man. We three are all your constituents, as are the*

150 or so people we represent, as the Residents' Association for the WH Village here. We're here because – I'm sure like many other WH sites – we are concerned about the idea that we might be sold off to a private equity firm. Unlike other sites, though, we do have an option open to us other than just to hope that the Authorities veto the take-over on competition grounds. We have a firm offer from the Charity set up by Ingham's Brewery for them to buy out the Village and, over many years, use it to house long-serving Ingham's staff in their retirement.

We've produced a little background brief, which we'll leave with you; and we won't infringe on your time by taking you through it now. Sufficient to say that, if WH will sell at anything like a sensible price, we have the funds available now and a management team ready and willing to take on this challenge. Existing leaseholders will see very little difference and will have a much easier time disposing of their leases when the time comes. Ingham's initiative will send a signal to all the remaining family and co-op firms out there in the country that this could be a brilliant new way for them to tackle the old age of long-serving employees. And you will have 150 happy constituents in the Home plus 1,000 or more Ingham's employee families in your constituency well disposed towards you. Good preparation for the next Election. If you agree that Ingham's initiative is worth supporting, what we want is for you to throw your considerable political muscle behind the takeover and help us persuade WH that selling this one site would help WH achieve what it wants to get."

The Minister smiled, thinly. *"I have been apprised of much of this argument already; and, of course, I'll look at anything you leave with me. I must say at the outset that I have cut myself out of Government decision loops on the takeover because of my mother. But I have let my Ministerial colleagues know what I think about our general policy in this area. That policy is wholly in line with Conservative thinking: i.e. that corporate restructurings are to be supported if actual and potential customers are properly protected. And we are certainly of the view that innovative ways of tackling the issues of old age, like this Ingham's Charity, deserve a try. I think all I can say is that I wish you well with your discussions with WH; and you can certainly say that is what I've told you, in those terms, when you see them."*

The Minister rose. He had obviously said all he was going to say. Deedes looked quickly at his 2 colleagues and nodded his head very slightly. They had got the best they could hope for. Time to go and take the battle on to WH.

15

That turned out to be easier said than done; and Deedes and his colleagues might have fallen at this hurdle had it not been for Fox's desire to keep everything in his own hands. Deedes arranged for the three of them to travel to Manchester and make their pitch to WH. But that pitch would have been to someone no more than halfway up the management chain, in the Finance Department. Fortunately for Deedes, Fox was requiring written notice to his office of any correspondence or event that might impact the deal and so Fox got to hear about the meeting several days before it was due to take place.

Even more fortunately for Deedes, Fox had an unexpected vacancy in his diary on the day of the meeting, as another meeting he had been due to have was cancelled at the last minute. Thus, rather to their surprise but considerable relief, Deedes and his colleagues found themselves in Fox's office, rather than in the bowels of the Accounting Department.

Deedes had agreed to lead for his side and, sensing what had happened and deducing Fox's probable paranoia, he immediately suggested that he and Fox should have a quick one-to-one meeting, so that *"we won't waste your time, Mr. Fox."*

Left to themselves, Deedes decided to be very blunt but to speak in words that, if later reported to a third-party, could not be twisted to a different meaning or could just be denied. *"Mr. Fox. The Retirement Village we live in is a minute part of the deal you are working on. But it matters a lot to us, for obvious reasons. Now, I can imagine how much time and effort you and WH must be putting into the deal; and so we're here today because we think we can help you unlock one key element and improve the chances of the whole deal being waived through by the Authorities. You see, we don't fancy being traded to Liford and we have an alternative buyer, in the form of the Charity financed by Ingham's Brewery, which is a big local employee where we are. We also want to keep the clinic and dementia services provided now by WH, which we value and which we know you want to keep providing elsewhere.*

Now, that would normally be neither here nor there for you; you can't be expected to go round your huge portfolio of sites and negotiate on them one by one. But we happen to have the ear of the Minister for Competition, for a reason I won't bother you with. And we know that he and his political colleagues are very keen in principle to see this one deal go through, so that Ingham's can own what in time will become a company-focused retirement home.

In part, I know that's because the Government hope that there are a lot of other big family firms out there who might do the same. And such an outcome looks well for the Tories' new desire to seem warm and cuddly to the masses. I would also be very naïve if I didn't acknowledge that the Minister's attitude had something to do with the number of Ingham's employees in his constituency. But what I can say, having met the Minister and talked it over with him, is that I would judge that you would get a very good return from him if you took the time to negotiate a price with us. We have the money and resources behind us, thanks to the Charity. We can pay you a fair price and we're not going to be infringing either on existing leaseholders' rights or on any key WH interest. Basically, my message to you is: pick one of your trusted staff to come and work a deal through with us. You won't regret it."

Fox said little but called the full meeting back and let Deedes lead them through the draft proposal. No more was said in the wider meeting about the Minister's interest. But, at the end, Fox did sum up by saying *"I'd like to thank Mr Deedes and his colleagues for their innovative proposal. At first sight, I can see some attractions for you and for Ingham's. I can also see that the idea might play well with the press, who don't seem to like Liford any more than you do. I'll certainly take soundings; and Martin here"* – he indicated the No. 2 in the Accounting Department who was sitting next to him in the meeting –*"will be in touch shortly. We would obviously have to be satisfied on price and that there were no loose ends that could come back to bite WH, if that's what loose ends can do. We should also want our lawyers to be very fully involved, to protect our interests. But"* – and he smiled benevolently at the hapless Martin – *"I'm sure Martin will enjoy a couple of days in the country air with you. And I can assure you he will keep me fully in touch with how things are going. I estimate that we have perhaps 8 more weeks to close off all the key elements of the deal. I'm sure this little wrinkle on the bigger picture can get wrapped up well within that time frame."*

16

Next day, Deedes, Victoria and Graham met up back 'home'. *"Very satisfactory, I thought"* said Victoria. *"I'm glad, John, you found such a good and early way to get Fox thinking about the political bonus of the deal. But we now are going to have to help the Charity wade through tons of legal and other guff. And, no doubt, Martin will want it to look as though he's striking a deal that he can represent back in Manchester as a win for WH."*

"Yes" said Graham *"But I can see that we have a lot of other stuff on our plate too. It's time to face up to our next 'big question'. What do we say to all the WH staff here? Word will surely spread quickly once Martin and some Head Office lackeys turn up to talk to us. And what do we ourselves want to do with the local staff? Keep them? Try to put them back to WH? Or what?*

It seems to me that we have to focus on not upsetting a potentially unstable ship. IF we get the deal we want, we have the Charity behind us with money and some useful staff and other resources of their own. But, at least initially, we will be very dependent on staff who know what they're doing, here in this Village. What to do if there's a fire, or a flood, how to keep the food rolling in the kitchen and so on. We're lucky that the initial teething problems of the opening are behind us. But it's very obvious that smooth running depends on a lot of technology working properly and, really, only the staff know much about that; just remember the incident we had with the underfloor heating about 6 weeks ago."

Victoria chipped in. *"Of course, you're right. But we do have quite a lot going for us. If we get the deal we want, WH will continue to run the Care Floor and the Dementia Ward. They'll have a close interest in helping us make sure the food keeps coming, for example. And no doubt, if we can be specific enough in advance, they'll probably also be quite happy to provide other services on a paid basis.*

The more important plus for us, I think, is that most of the staff here are NOT people who have worked for WH for years, so they probably won't worry too much if they get a decent offer from the Charity to replace their WH package. Also, I know from talking to some of them that many are either local people or have moved into the region to take this job up. They won't want to up sticks again unless they really have no choice. And, finally on the same track, the Ingham's Charity probably has as good a reputation as any employer they are likely to find. What I think we need to do is to decide, I admit it will be on an incomplete basis because we haven't known them for long, which of the current key staff here we want to keep; and then, with the Charity's help put a package together for each of them. One really good thing – we know their current salaries can't be great; no-one gets paid that much in this sector except people like the Liford management. And, as a fall-back, if there really is a key WH employee we can't attract, let's see if we can negotiate say a 1 year 'lease' for them from WH. "

John and Graham readily agreed this plan. The allocation of responsibilities barely needed discussion. Each knew that Deedes was the prime lead for everything on finance, Graham led on everything else that involved the Charity and Victoria was prime lead for relations with leaseholders and, now they agreed, staff.

17

Victoria arranged a meeting with the WH Manager of the Village, for the next morning. The woman was relatively young – mid-30s Victoria thought – and, importantly, not a WH lifer. Rather, the woman had clearly seen the appointment as Village Manager as an important step up in her career and was determined to make it work. Victoria also knew that the woman was (relatively) a local, so hopefully Ingham's and its Charity would seem at least as familiar as WH. So far, her record as Manager had – as the residents saw it – been patchy. But Victoria thought this was largely down to 2 factors. The woman was still learning her job and, hopefully, would get better; and WH seemed to give her very little autonomy. Take away the WH machine and she might perform much better, though she would also be much more exposed.

Victoria decided to adopt Deede's style and go straight to the point with the Manager. "*Sue, I wanted to bring you up to date with events. You've heard about the proposed WH-Liford deal and I'm sure you and your colleagues here must be feeling a bit uneasy. Well, I'm here to tell you that the Residents' Association has come up with quite a different idea, which is that this Village gets sold by WH to the local Ingham's Charity. They would use it, over the years, as a Home for their longer-serving retired employees. In the meantime, all the existing leaseholders here would carry on as now. WH would carry on running the Clinic and Dementia Wards. You, if you are willing, would stay on as Manager, responsible to Ingham's. You would become an Ingham's Charity employee on the same or better terms than you have now with WH. I can already say that, in respect of pensions, the Ingham package I know is considerably better than the one you are currently on.*

I can't tell you much about how the Village would develop in these circumstances. But I think I can say with some certainty that we would give you much more autonomy and local freedom of decision-making than WH do now. And, in some ways, your job would become less complex – for example, no more endless efforts to sell apartments because the Charity would be handling all that. What you wouldn't have is access to WH's knowledge of retirement, their lawyers or their accountants. You ***would*** *have the Charity's legal and accounting support; and I can assure you that you would have us in the Resident's Association guarding your back and giving you all the support we could. But there's no doubting it would be a rather different world for you.*

Now, let's kick the idea around and see what your initial reaction is. I have no guarantee that WH will play ball. But we can make it worth their while to do so and a small WH team will be coming from Head Office in the next couple of days to kick the process off. Whatever your initial reaction now, we need to brief the staff here before Head Office arrives. We can't afford to have staff leaving because they are uncertain about their future. And we can NOW offer jobs with certainty with Ingham's Charity if the deal goes ahead, to almost everyone who is here other than those covered by the Clinic and Dementia Wards. Their jobs will continue as is with WH, just as now. The only job I think we can't guarantee is the job selling new apartments; but, had things gone to plan, those would anyway have been sold by now. And the chances must be, if the salesman is good, he will already have a new job half-lined up."

18

For the three residents at the centre of this mini-storm, the days seemed to pass all too quickly. As Graham remarked to Deedes at one point "*Thank goodness we're retired and don't have much else on that needs doing. But, and I guess this is just us getting old, I can't face meetings, lawyers, and all the rest like I used to. Thank goodness that there should only be a few weeks at this pace – the WH-Liford deal presumably must close soon if it is going to happen at all.*"

They had an arrangement to meet every Monday morning, just the three of them, to check that things were going to plan and agree a line on any issues likely to come up during the week. The rest of the Residents' Association Committee had made it clear, from the outset, that this was all too much for them.

A month into the process, and most lights were green. Deedes kicked off as he always did at the Monday meeting. *"The WH team will be back again this week. I think we're making good progress. Certainly, they've accepted that they are not going to get sued by existing angry leaseholders for the change of ownership. As one of them said in an unguarded moment – 'if I had to choose between being owned by a brewery and Lifords, I know which I'd choose'. I've avoided saying that, if we're really pushed, we'll go to £7 million or more. I think that's something we can keep off the table for now; but it might be the deciding factor to get their accountant on-side. If we let him come up with that figure right at the end, he can present it to Fox to show how he, Martin, has added value for WH. And WH seem totally happy to quote us for any back-up services we seem to need; we haven't had nearly as much kick-back from them as I thought we would get. I suspect Lifords are keeping them pretty busy."*

"The Charity Trustees are OK too" added Graham. *"Their lawyers are a bit of hard work but I can see most of this is totally new to them and they have to be able to reassure the Trustees it's all going to work. And one big unexpected plus. The Trustees have said that, if they take us over, they'll give all the residents the 10% discount on their drink products that all their staff and retirees get now. That's gone down very well among some of the leaseholders here; and not just the men."*

Victoria rounded off. *"I certainly don't want to spoil the party atmosphere. Things are OK on my front too. We have stirred up quite a few suggestions from leaseholders about things we might do here in future. But several of those ideas, like having a small grocery shop and finding a bank to come in, say one afternoon a week, are worth pursuing anyway. As for the staff,*

I think most of them will give us a try. The Manager's certainly on board and I suspect most of the local staff think that, if we take over and it doesn't work out, they can get another local job pretty easily, given how little unemployment there is around here."

19

Fox's forecast that there were 8 more weeks to go had proved wrong but not by a serious amount. Just 11 weeks after Fox had said it, all the parties were gathered in the Village itself, to sign off on the transfer of the Village to Ingham's.

The Minister looked quickly round and checked that everyone who needed to be there was present. He then launched off without further ado. The room was far from ideal for its present purpose and there were at least 3 too many people in it; but he needed to press on. The Minister – and, quite separately, Deedes too – had, for several days, had this nagging feeling that it wouldn't take much for the whole deal to come unstitched.

"As I think you all know, I am James Deacon. I am the Minister for Consumers and Competition in the Conservative

Government. I'll leave the rest of you to introduce yourselves if there is a need. But I want to stress that this is very much a non-meeting. We are all here today for different purposes; I am making a visit in my constituency and we all happen to find ourselves able to gather briefly for a chat now about our mutual interests. At the end of this non-meeting, we can agree a short non-statement that we can use as briefing if needed. Now, on my left…"

The tall sparse figure next to Deacon took up the line. ""*As you all know, I am John Deedes, chair of the Four Winds company which will take over this Retirement Village on behalf of the Ingham's Brewery Charity. I'm very grateful to the Minister and indeed all the others of you present for being here.*

My two co-directors of The Four Winds here and I are present with just one purpose. To buy this Retirement Village lock stock and barrel from its current owners, WH. As most of you know, we have had months of discussion with WH. I can only stress that we have no interest in any other WH or Liford asset and that we have the necessary agreements and, of course, the cleared bank funds ready this moment to seal our purchase. We want to agree a deal now, our plans have been on hold for far too long now. It is really only feasible for us, in the time available, to buy from WH as we have already negotiated with them all the necessary elements of support that WH will need to provide in the early months to help us do this right.

And," Deedes looked long and hard at the Minister *"we would strongly prefer the deal to be done today. That suits us. I understand that it suits WH; and I think the Minister would find it helpful too, given that the main local paper's print deadline is noon tomorrow. As part of our efforts to get this deal over the line, I can confidently say that the press reaction will be* very *favourable to the Minister ahead of what we all expect to be a very close Election when it is called. A stand alone and fully satisfactory solution to the fate of 150 elderly people living here, one partially facilitated by the Minister himself – as we have agreed it should be presented – should read very well I think."*

Liford's team was headed by Frank Brightwell, whom Fox had not seen or spoken to since Brightwell had threatened him with Caroline's pictures. He, pitched in at that point, although the WH people were next round the table. *"We'll be on our way. I think. We understand that the political complexities of the approvals needed for our buying what WH want to sell. We're delighted as we understand the Minister's colleagues have signed off on the whole WH/Liford deal. We have no problem with WH selling this one property – or indeed of it giving the thing away, if that's what they want. So we'll come back later and get together with WH in a few minutes for the big deal."* With that, the Liford 4 – Brightwell, lawyer, press girl and general dogsbody – upped and left. Which in one throw dealt with the overcrowding.

For a minute, no-one left said anything. Then the WH CEO Marcus Fox, who had been delighted to see the back of Brightwell at least for the time being, stirred himself into action. *"I hope WH's position is very clear. We are ready to complete the deal today with Mr. Deedes and his colleagues. I understand, from my Finance colleague here, that a final price has been agreed for the Village. The hugely much larger WH/Liford deal has been ready to sign for several days. So, as far as we are concerned, we just need the signatures of the Ingham's Trustees and Mr. Deedes and his colleagues to action this part of the deal. And then we can finalise with Liford. We have seen, and are quite happy with, the document being put out by the Ministers' colleagues on their agreement to the competition aspects of the whole deal going ahead. The last few weeks have been hard work for a lot of people. For WH, I know the deal makes sense. Liford, I'm sure feel the same for their part. And I can only wish Mr. Deedes and his associates all the best for their entry to the world of retirement, as we leave it."*

20

The ready availability of tea or coffee at any time of day or night is one of the things you can be certain to find in a Retirement Village or Care Home. As the local WH staff were clearly in awe of having the CEO of the company present in the Village, a couple of junior staff were quickly found loitering near the Activities Room where the meeting had taken place and dispatched to provide the (mostly coffee) needs of those who were staying on. Word that the deal was 'on' would be round the Village in minutes.

The formal signatures took only a moment, with Fox signing for WH and Deedes plus one of the Ingham's Charity Trustees for the purchasers. Both sets of lawyers present then insisted on each of the many pages of text being initialled by the 3 signatories, a process which took far longer. Finally, the local newspaper photographer was allowed in and Fox, Deedes and the Trustee all joined in what would look in the press photo like a mass signing by all the parties involved. For this one photo, the Minister took up a central position behind the signatories. Deedes imagined that the Minister had already agreed the headline to go with it in tomorrow's paper. He himself had already provided a short interview to the local journalist running the story. She, in turn, had been pretty optimistic that at least one of the big daily nationals would run the story too. As she murmured to Deedes "*A lot of people drink Ingham's and everyone will like a story about loyal old employees getting a decent home for life.*"

When this was all done, Deedes rose and shuffled his papers together. "*Mr. Fox. We'll leave you now to sign your mega deal with Liford. I understand that at least 2 of the national papers are here for that signing. And I saw your staff wheeling in some champagne earlier, so I trust you will be able to celebrate in the style you want. This won't be the last time that your staff will be here, by a long chalk, given the elements in our Agreement about the on-going nursing and support services you will be providing. But you should know that so far your people have done an excellent job and I'd like to record our thanks to them. They will continue to be very welcome. Now, my colleagues and I need to reassure our leaseholders and staff that the deal is done and that their future is secure. I think we shall make do with prosecco and Ingham's beer, rather than champagne, but that will be drunk with good cheer, I'm confident. Free and regular alcohol will be a feature of our on-going relationship with our leaseholders. If WH were ever going to get back in the retirement world, which I'm sure they have no plans to do, the value of free alcohol for good relations is something I would stress to you all. From what I've heard of Liford, the word 'free' is not one they regularly use. But it takes all sorts. And we are just delighted to be facing the freedom to make our own choices in future."*

21

The rest of the play panned out as intended. Fox found he didn't actually have to speak to Brightwell, just co-sign various papers evidencing the deal. Without looking too sour about it, Fox shared a glass of champagne with Brightwell after the signing and took part in the necessary press pictures. But the primary focus for both WH and Liford was the national press and that required one-on-one briefings not a shared platform. Fox felt a growing sense of elation as the morning progressed. The deal was done. His no doubt substantial bonus from a grateful Board had been as good as promised. And, although the way Caroline had treated him still hurt, overall life felt pretty good. Even the news that Brightwell was becoming CEO of the Care Home conglomerate didn't faze him. He, Fox, had seen enough of Care Homes and the like never to wish to see another for the rest of his life, if possible. Brightwell, Ingham's and this man Deedes were all welcome to what they had signed up for.

The press reaction of the next few days also gave everybody what they had hoped for. The Minister got his local 'good news' out. The WH share price was favoured with a rise of about 7% when the deal was confirmed and, more important for Fox, there were 2 Sunday paper articles the next weekend about how WH was entering a new and very positive phase of its business life. Fox had been interviewed for both and had made no effort to play down how much he personally had been involved in getting the deal done. The elderly living in the Retirement Villages and Care Homes got precisely no coverage from anyone, exactly what they could reasonably have expected.

Life continued in that happy vein for just a week. And what caused it to falter was something out of left field that Fox in his wildest nightmares would never have thought up. When he had first faced up to what Caroline and Liford had done, he had worried about what would happen if the story leaked. But he had been clear in his own mind that Liford had no reason to do that, as he – Fox – had every intention of pushing the deal through. And so it had proved. So, surely this would just remain a little local secret.

What he could not have forecast was the police raid on Caroline's flat which threw up copies of the photos of Fox with her. Caroline had made the mistake – no doubt at Liford's bidding – of trying the same trick she had pulled on Fox with a CEO who was made of much sterner stuff than Fox had been. As he was a major supplier to the Met Police, this man had got some excellent police contacts; and the police were happy to help a major supplier to investigate what appeared to be a prima facie case of blackmail.

And had not the police been as leaky as they often are, they might not have subsequently slipped copies of Caroline's extensive photograph collection to a journalist, telling her that she was welcome to identify the people and do what she wanted with the result. The net effect of all this, though, and even given that Fox was only a minor 'major' figure was that Fox's name leaked out in the press about a week later, together with some very splendid photos. With the news quickly came speculation about how the Caroline/Fox 'liaison' as the papers called it had been tied in with the deal with Liford. And, while nothing was available from Caroline's flat that could prove much on that score, the implication/smear was very quickly drawn that the deal had not been 'unconnected' with the liaison. In short, Fox was finished.

His Chairman had used exactly that term – 'finished' – when he had confronted Fox the day after the story had broken. After a few hours' agonised thinking, Fox had readily accepted that he would agree without further ado to the deal the Chairman offered to minimise the adverse effects on WH – namely that Fox would resign with immediate effect to 'pursue other interests'. Of course, the Chairman would do more; the firm's Magic Circle lawyers would pick up a good few million to conduct an independent review of Fox's doings for a start. But the Chairman had been sufficiently in touch with the deal from the outset to know it was very unlikely that Fox had in any way damaged WH's interests in the deal; it had self-evidently been a good one for WH, as testified at the time by their own advisers. What was critical now – as the Chairman saw it – was to cut Fox's links with WH, so that – if Fox ever had to appear as a witness in what might be a far-reaching blackmail case – WH's involvement would be second-hand and part of corporate history.

For Fox personally, the days flew by and the blows of fate descended on him in quick succession. His wife, not surprisingly, threw him out and he quickly ended up living with a married daughter about 20 minutes from home. His lawyer suggested that, financially, the divorce would be a one-way procession of assets from him to his wife. His days emptied out. There was nothing to do. And nearly all his so-called business friends faded immediately from view. The few who didn't disappear provided little comfort, with their set defensive faces, and endless tiptoeing round his 'problem'.

Within a month, Fox found himself reaching for the whisky every night. The only thing he had going for him, apart from his daughter's support (which had been surprising but very welcome), was that the WH share price continued to climb, unaffected it seemed by his departure. All the shares he had acquired as part of the management incentive schemes in WH he had been on for the last 20 years (and unaffected by his rapid departure) could now be sold off at a very good price. He had lost any chance of a bonus for the deal. Nevertheless, so far as he could see, there would still be money for the whisky, even after the divorce, at least for a good length of time.

Caroline's experiences during that period were rather more fraught. Initially, there had been several days of intensive questioning from the police, adrenaline still high from finding such a marvellous set of photographs in the raid. Caroline had had the sense immediately to deny anything that the photos themselves did not yield. Her liaison with Fox, for example, had been personal not 'corporate'. *"I got to know Fox when we started casting an eye over WH. I liked him and one thing led to another. No, I never attempted to ask for money from Fox. No, my employers didn't know I was sleeping with him."* The Liford lawyers – the best in this kind of business and all too familiar with what Liford did and wanted – leapt to her defence.

They grilled Caroline to help strengthen the weakest parts of her defence. They also made sure, by the time the police got to them, that the other men in the photos all joined the chorus to argue that, for them, Caroline had been personal not corporate; and they were, happily, all able to corroborate Caroline's own bank statement that no money had ever changed hands. The men themselves – Fox included – all found this line of defence acceptable – of course, there had never been any suggestion of blackmail. They had, after all, each found Caroline's charms irresistible at the time; and, happily for their egos, Caroline had fallen for them each in turn. Fox certainly had no intention of mentioning the once made threat that he had received. Only one of the men was forced out from his company, for having an affair, as Fox had been. For the rest, it was history already.

As for the man who had launched this tsunami of action through his contacts at the Met, even he lost interest as soon as he had got his own photos back. His name was successfully kept out of the papers; and he certainly had no desire to bring an action against Caroline or Liford (who by this time had gone on the offensive and were threatening libel actions against anyone claiming that Liford had ever done anything wrong). When the time came, the Director of Public Prosecutions had no hesitation in concluding that it would not be in the public interest to bring a case. Six months later, as Fox often ruefully thought in later life, the only flotsam left lying around were those wretched photos – which, for him at least, would never vanish.

Once the police enquiry had ended, Caroline reached a reasonably amicable settlement with Liford who, though they had stood by her, needed her continuing silence and could see little use for her, now that she was publically marked. Last heard of, she had moved to the Middle East where rumour had it she was 'facilitating' the introduction of young women into several of a local Sheik's harems on remunerative terms.

Perhaps the most affected person in the long-run – though for no very good reason – was Frank Brightwell. It wasn't a question of losing Caroline, though he had always enjoyed having her round. But, as Brightwell got used to the issues likely to face the estate his company had now taken over, he came increasingly to dislike his new job, despite its higher status within Liford. And, every 2 or 3 months, he would see another article about the origins and the growing success of The Four Winds, nearly always drawn to highlight the differences between a caring Charity and an uncaring private equity firm.

Within a year, Brightwell had played all the usual tricks in the Liford playbook in his new empire. He had been only a bit player a few years earlier, when a large company had been loaded with billions of debt and stripped of almost the same amount of cash in dividends to the private equity owners, before the company was launched back on mug punters. But he had learned the lessons well. So, large amounts of high-rate fixed debt had been issued, secured on the freeholds of the retirement sites; and that money had quickly been passed to Liford and the other shareholders by way of large dividends. Liford had then sold out of as many shares as they could, meaning that, overall, they had made money even if the empire subsequently collapsed.

Brightwell had always thought of retirement sites as cash cows and he now found numerous ways of wringing a little more milk out of each udder. Monthly bills had always been due by the middle of the following month; now they were due a week before the beginning of the next month. The alcohol stocks in the Care Home bars were fortified by brands with some link to Liford and the price of, say, a G & T raised by 30p a time. So it went on. But Brightwell could never feel anything other than that he hated the job; and he came –over time – to blame Ingham's and Deedes personally for every problem or bit of bad publicity that he, Brightwell, encountered.

22

The Directors of the Four Winds had seen the juicy story about the photographs appear straight after the raid. But it had concerned them very little and worried them not at all. Rather, every sinew they had was being dedicated to keeping the Four Winds from being struck by unwelcome storms from elsewhere, of which there were plenty.

The WH staff that the Four Winds had taken on proved to be like rabbits in front of a fast moving car when they actually had the authority, indeed the need, to decide things for themselves on the spot. Up to that point, it had always been safe – indeed required – that they pass every question to someone at Head Office. That was no longer possible.

Staff numbers at the Village were also always an issue.

The Village was in an area of almost zero unemployment. Turn-over for the whole industry was something like 30% a year and The Four Winds faced more than that in their first year of operation. And Liford made things worse, after Brightwell's dislike of The Four Winds had solidified into a grinding permanency. Liford had 3 homes within 10 miles of The Four Winds; and each was instructed by Brightwell personally to try and attract away the better staff from The Four Winds.

The 3 resident directors also found themselves drawn into every 'local' dispute that sprang up like weeds in the Village. Fifty of the residents had been keen gardeners for most of their lives. Now, each had their own personal plans for reorganising the planting in the grounds. Food also gave rise to endless dispute. The vegetables were overcooked, the portions were too large or too small; the plates were too hot, the food was too cold. *"And, you know, Mr. Deedes, I fed a very demanding household for 30 years. I really think I know more about makes a good bubble and squeak than your chef."* So it went on.

There were then the tensions between the small but growing number of Ingham's retirees and those who had bought in initially. These tensions, it quickly became apparent, were class based and came to a head in what became known locally as the 'washing line saga'. The new arrivals were used to hanging their washing out on a line; the original buyers were outraged at the thought that washing could possibly sully the communal view as they walked around the grounds. Leases were waved around and legal action threatened. Several confrontations followed around the washing lines, with both sides of course certain that they were in the right. Deedes eventually managed to broker a 'deal' by which a small part of the grounds near where the newcomers lived in the Village were fenced off from prying eyes to allow washing to be dried in the sun. A kind of kitchen garden, as Deedes himself put it.

The attention of the original leaseholders was also helpfully diverted by a number of schemes that had been suggested during the move to independence and several of which, as it happened, were announced the same week as the new drying area. The local Council was persuaded, after considerable effort, to put its mobile library in the Village once a week. A small area in the main building was set aside to allow a small shop to be opened for a couple of hours, four days a week, to sell basics. Deedes often found himself serving in the shop, so acute sometimes was the staff shortage. But a local convenience store run by a cheerful Asian found and brought the stock, so overall it was an idea that worked.

The one 'improvement' that had widely been asked for which proved impossible to engineer was having a local bank open on the premises a couple of days a week. None of the major banks that they approached could see the value of having effectively monopoly access to 150 elderly and often quite wealthy people. As one local branch manager put it to Deedes during a heated discussion – modern technology could meet most banking needs if only the (wretched) customers involved would just learn to use it.

Each of the 3 resident Directors found that the work load never seemed to slacken much. After one particularly trying week, Deedes – who had forced himself to spend the week steeped in classes at the spa and a huge list of 'organised' activities to see more of daily life there – found that his sole (awful pun coming) journal record of note had been a poem that he'd written about the food which, by now, he had come to have his own very strong views on too:

Battered haddock; battered cod.
I tell you now I swear by God
If it appears on Friday's menu
I'm eating at another venue.

Fridays now, for a whole year
'Batter's' on there, made with beer.
The fish inside is often small
Sometimes almost none at all.

Give us salmon, give us hake
Any change and no mistake.
I know what's coming! Yes, it's new
Battered cod done as a stew!

Something was telling him he needed to stop what he was doing!

23

Before Deedes could do anything to change his circumstances, Brightwell launched what he had worked out should be a killer blow. Things like trying to bid away key staff from Four Winds had been fun but were clearly never going to land a knock-out blow. What Brightwell needed was something that undermined the finances of the new entity; and, at first sight, this had looked pretty difficult to arrange. The Four Winds just wasn't subject to the same financial pressures as a normal retirement home, because of the queue of Inghams' employees waiting to retire there. You could only land a knockout blow on that if you could choke off the money from the Ingham's charity.

You could only do that if you controlled Ingham's…

You could only do that if you bought the Ingham's company…

And you could only do that if you had some kind of story to tell in the market…

Which was just the kind of thing, Brightwell realised when the obvious hit him, that Lifords was set up to do.

Lifords, like most private equity firms, had its core company from which Brightwell had come. But its main purpose was to provide money and people to whichever of Liford's corporate vehicles needed them to tie up the latest deal. So, Brightwell was CEO of the new Care Homes conglomerate but he was still, first and foremost, a Liford's man. And, as such, he had no problem in getting a small team of Liford analysts to investigate the Ingham's company in depth as the first step to choking off the flow of money from the charity (or, as the analysts thought, to launch a bid for Ingham's).

Ingham's was a publicly quoted company and so Liford's had no problem in establishing where the shareholdings lay. Two Ingham brothers had run the company for about 20 years ago and each held about 15% of the shares, either in their own name or in family trusts which they controlled. The brothers were now reaching retirement age; and the Liford analysts had easily established that there were no next generation Inghams to take over. So, in theory, there were 2 blocks of shares that might well be up for sale at the right price. Otherwise, the shares were widely held, with a dozen pension funds and asset managers holding 3-5% each plus around 20% held by what was assumed to be private individuals, often –it was claimed – loyal Ingham beer drinkers.

In recent years, the shares had gone nowhere, though they had provided a regular 4% or so annual dividend yield. In short, the shares were seen in the market as a classic defensive stock – but this at a time (as the WH deal had shown) when the market found growth stories potentially much more interesting.

Brightwell had also had the analysts dig into the Ingham's Charity, given that his whole purpose was to throttle The Four Winds' finances at source. This time, it was the Charity Commission returns that provided most of the necessary information. Not for the first time, Brightwell found himself thankful for the fact that private equity firms had to provide next to no information about themselves, in huge contrast to publicly quoted companies or charities. Here, again, the news was basically what he wanted to hear. The Charity's income came from a percentage of Ingham's profits and the return on a very limited endowment it held in its own right. Whoever owned Ingham's controlled the money paid in from the company to the Charity. And whoever owned Ingham's could – within 18 months – both turn off the income tap and nominate a majority of Trustees to the Charity. If Brightwell could get 51% of Ingham's shares (preferably 70% but 51% would do at a pinch), Brightwell could get The Four Winds where he wanted it inside 2 years.

From past experience, Brightwell knew that new deals like this were best not rushed. Roughly half the large corporate shareholders in Ingham's were run by people that Brightwell knew personally. They would understand a nuanced tip at the right time that a bid would shortly be forthcoming and that Lifords would welcome their voting for the deal. Nothing that could be picked up after the event or, just as bad from Liford's point of view, nothing to push the price up ahead of the bid. After all, Brightwell needed a story for his own financiers that a bid would make Liford money, even if –for once – that thought was not top of his own list. So, he still had to make the numbers stack up for the people who really called the shots in Liford, if a bid was to proceed.

Over the next four weeks, Brightwell arranged a meal or drinks with a total of 8 fund managers. Each was told that, if they held onto their stake in Ingham's a bid was likely to come and take them out at a nice profit. So, it was worth holding on. Each was also politely reminded that, thanks to London Stock Exchange rules, Brightwell knew to the last share what their holding in Ingham's was currently; any further increase in the holding would be taken as 'unfriendly' by Lifords (because it could push the share price up) and paid back in spades sometime in the future. The message was in every case taken and heeded.

Brightwell also had Caroline's replacement (Caroline had been too useful for Liford to lose both in person and in the function she had served). The replacement – Cheryl – was tasked to get close to the Inghams' family, especially the 2 brothers, to see how best their 30% of the shares could be won round. That, in fact, required little more than a minor flirtation with one of the next generation of Inghams. From that, Cheryl was quickly able to confirm that there was indeed no next generation of Inghams to leap to the company's rescue; and, more usefully, that the 2 brothers did not get on well with each other. Twenty years together in management had strained the family ties between them considerably. So, the older was making no secret of his intention to retire to somewhere in the sun (*"with a tax haven in easy reach"* added one of the third generation waspishly to Cheryl). And the other wanted to liquidate his Ingham's holding to fulfil a lifetime's ambition to buy up a majority stake in the local English Football League club that was known to be on offer and that he had supported all his life. *"We're talking League Division 2 here"* said Cheryl in one of her reports to Brightwell. *"But his 15% of Ingham's will do that nicely – as well as pay off the Inghams on his side of the family. Make the offer a decent one first time round and you'll be laughing."*

Brightwell, however, had more trouble than he had expected putting together a plausible story for the bidders. As with WH, Brightwell ran his eye over each of the national breweries, to see which might plausibly be able to cut costs when taking Ingham's over. There were two UK brewers that might fit; and one of them openly aspired to becoming a bigger fish than they were already AND had a CEO who clearly wanted, as had Fox, to lead his troops to new heights.

Brightwell then worked on a scenario in which a US brewer could plausibly claim interest in Ingham's suite of specialist ales. (It turned out that California was having one of its periodic 'love-ins' with British real ale so that part of the story book was relatively easy to fill in.) And the US parent of Lifords had no trouble in turning up a California-based brewer who was willing to come in and play up the potential of Ingham's specialist beers in the US.

Even so, Brightwell found it much harder than he had expected to conjure up numbers that would look plausible in a prospectus and which would justify a bid for Ingham's well above its present level. And Cheryl had stressed that this was a 'must' if the older brother's shares were to be obtained.

Plans for the bid crept forward. Brightwell got to befriend the CEO of the potential bidder; after all, he had to be sure that the man would play ball with Brightwell's plans to get hold of the Ingham's charity. At this point, Cheryl was 'utilised' to make sure the man would continue to see things the way Brightwell did; and Brightwell certainly felt better once he had seen the photos that Cheryl kindly provided, that would constitute the insurance on the CEO. But, as with Fox, he didn't think it would ever come to that.

24

The first that Deedes knew of what was in the wind was the announcement of the bid; as usual with such things this came out at 7a.m. in a Stock Exchange announcement. Lifords didn't feature much in the supporting text. But they were, naturally, cited as advisers to the bidders and as the potential source of much of the bid's funding. Deedes saw that and very quickly worked out the similarity between this and the WH bid. He then started to take the deal apart and ask himself what downside, if any, there could be for The Four Winds, if the bid succeeded.

Of course, Lifords could just be in it to make money. But – and when Deedes raised it later that day with Graham – the latter agreed that, if it was a coincidence, it was a strange one. Nobody in the market had talked seriously about a bid for Ingham's for years; though you could argue that the retirement of the 2 brothers running the company did make some such move more plausible. Both Deedes and Graham were vaguely aware that Brightwell didn't like them – the attempted poaching of staff had made that clear. But surely a firm like Lifords had better things to do than pursue small petty grievances, especially if that were likely to take time, money and effort? So, what was the true purpose of the bid?

Deedes still had a few contacts in the City and his first step was to check if they could throw any light on the bid. The answer was basically 'no. What he did establish, though, was that – as things stood – the bid was likely to succeed. Ingham's share price rose after the bid was announced, to just under the bid price. And Deedes knew, without having to be told, that this meant no-one was seriously expecting a higher counter bid (or the Ingham's price would have gone above the bid). It also meant that the market expected the bid to succeed (if not, the price would have headed back down towards where it was when the bid was made).

Graham was able, for his part, to dig around with other members of the Ingham family and establish the likely course of the 2 15% stakes held by the brothers. That quickly yielded the information that both stakes would likely be sold to Lifords. The only glimmer of comfort came from the mass of Ingham's private shareholders, who very clearly didn't want anything about the company to change and organised a 'protect our beer' website and did their best to make a fuss. But that, by itself wasn't going to change the outcome even if all those private shareholders voted against the bid.

Deedes, Graham and Victoria chewed the problem over from every angle they could think of. As far as they could see, if Lifords won Ingham's there would be nothing to stop them from cutting the flow of profits to the Charity and, maybe, that was what was intended. Less for the Charity meant more for the shareholders. So the Charity was at risk whether Lifords had it in for The Four Winds or not, as it was doubtful if Lifords would feel constrained for a minute from getting hold of money that could go to their shareholders .

"Well" concluded Deedes after the third long meeting between the 3 of them in a week *"we have to do something. I don't like it but it seems to me that the only chance we have of stopping this bid is an appeal to the Minister. There must be regional and other competitive issues at stake, if a national brewer is to take over Ingham's. And there'll be a groundswell of public sympathy for Ingham's – against Liford and a West Coast US brewer. Surely, he can make something of that. Victoria, do you think you can see what the Minister's mother might be willing to say to her son? We have no proof but I think it wouldn't be at all unreasonable for you to sell her the idea that, if she wants peace here in her last years, it would be a good idea if the Competition people intervene and either stop this bid or impose conditions on it that will frighten Liford away."*

Deedes didn't feel happy even suggesting that much. But he consoled himself that Liford – the "enemy" – had already shown themselves capable of doing much worse.

Victoria reported back several days later that the meeting with the Minister's mother had gone well.

And then everything went very quiet, with the national news being filled increasingly with the global spread of Covid19 and very little else. On March 11th 2020, the UK Government called for all non-essential travel and contact to stop; and on the same day the Competition Agency put out a short statement that they would be referring the Ingram's takeover for further review. The Minister had delivered.

After that, things moved incredibly quickly. Brightwell had initially been hugely annoyed by the Government announcement. But, fortunately for him, his lawyers hadn't drawn up a public protest against the decision before, on March 15th, all pubs were summarily closed by the Government. Brightwell worked out, within minutes, that this change would make the takeover of Ingham's a disastrously expensive move and, so, needed somehow to be avoided. Thus, when the Liford legal document eventually appeared a week later, the message was a very different one to what Brightwell had originally intended. It now read 'Liford has seen the Competition Authority's ruling on the proposed takeover of Ingham's by the UK brewer who is our client. We are confident that the investigation would show no changes were required to the bid. However, in the circumstances, the bidders are withdrawing their provisional offer, so no further action by the Competition Authority will be required.' Quite by chance, as Brightwell would admit years later and when he felt sure he was surrounded by friends, Liford had been saved by the government lockdown from what would almost certainly have been their most unsuccessful take-over ever. His lawyers had been adamant that, without the lockdown, the Takeover Panel would have insisted on the bid going ahead. Quite unintentionally, the Minister had saved Brightwell's bacon.

25

Deedes, Victoria and Paul had rather mixed feelings when they looked back. One uncomfortable fact hit them immediately. If Ingham's could only sell beer through supermarkets and on-line, income and profitability would take a huge hit while the lockdown lasted. So, the right hands might still be on the tiller so far as control of the Charity was concerned. But 5% of nothing, if there were no profits, was nothing. And the Four Winds had not been designed to stand on its own. The budget had been built around its receiving a regular stream of money from the Charity as more Ingham's retirees moved in. Only time could tell how that would play out but it caused the Directors considerable worry when they had time to raise their heads from the day job.

And that was the second blow, which first became apparent as soon deaths from the virus started escalating. Everywhere there were congregations of elderly people, they were sitting ducks for the virus; and precautionary measures made unheard of demands on staff, suppliers (and finances) that became ever more complex and pressing as the weeks went by.

Looking back, Deedes blamed himself for not having seen sooner the implications of the virus spreading. *" I was so wrapped up in seeing the bid off, I didn't spend nearly enough time thinking about where we'd get PPE from or any of the problems we've grappled with since"* he remarked over a late evening drink with Victoria after they had both completed a 12 hour shift helping the exhausted regular staff. *"And, if I'm honest, I don't think I could have wrapped my mind round most of the issues anyway. Before March. PPE to me meant only Philosophy, Politics and Economics at Oxford; not how were we to get hold of 1,000 safety aprons by Friday, in a world where every available piece of kit was being fought over tooth and nail."*

By the time, the first major lockdown was lifted, Deedes still blamed himself. But even he could see that the Four Winds also had a huge amount to be thankful for. Above all else, the virus had been kept out, though some of the homes nearby had not been so lucky and had suffered numerous resident deaths. The staff in the Village had stuck to a very unenviable job, often moving into the Village to reduce contamination risk. Staff resignations actually fell by around 80% during the worst of the crisis. Ingham's Charity had continued to come up with whatever money was needed without a murmur; and many of Ingham's own contacts also came up trumps – filling in gaps in food supplies, for example, often with delicacies like fresh-grown asparagus from local allotments. Even WH helped out, though Deedes suspected that someone in WH had carefully forgotten to mention that, for example, the WH-run Clinic Ward in the Four Winds couldn't possibly have needed 800 safety aprons for each week the lock-down lasted and that roughly 400 a week had found their way to the main care staff. But, and he was too young to have experienced The Second World War, Deedes guessed that this was just the kind of thing that went on behind even the best run and intentioned bureaucracy when everyone realised that the crisis had to be managed, whatever it took. And just as well that it did.

But what was clear, to Deedes at least, was that a vast amount was going to change as the economy struggled back towards some form of normality; and that the whole care home sector would itself see massive transformation. *"And"* as he said one evening over a drink with the other Directors *"I'm afraid I'm not up for that. I'm nearly 75 and the 6 months of lockdown have drained me completely. I think you both have coped brilliantly. But I just need to get out of your way and spend whatever time I have left doing and thinking about some of the simpler things of life. We've talked before about ensuring there's good succession; and now at least the Charity Trustees know what they're doing and the management here are a lot more use than they were 6 months ago. I'll give 6 months notice to make it easier; and I'm happy to help with what I'm sure will be the first big thing on your 'to-do' list. That is namely to work out how we're going to survive the period where Ingham's profits (and thus our income from that source) are diddly-squat. I'm sure we can do it. The likes of Liford care homes have far worse to look forward to, though I shan't lose any sleep over that.*

By the way, I did want to mention one thing. I've been approached by one of the better papers to speak at a retirement conference in a couple of months. 'How will our business model look in the new world?, that kind of thing. It'll probably be mostly Zoom based; and it may all feel rather odd, especially if I'm lecturing a nearly empty room. But it's how I want to go out. And I promise there'll be nothing libellous or that ties you guys in any way. Now let's have another drink as this bar is finally open properly."

26

The day of the conference swung round pretty quickly. Deedes had spoken in public regularly for over 40 years but, as he mounted the rostrum that morning– his was the first speech after the mid-morning coffee break – he felt twinges of anxiety. This really was 'it', the end of his lifetime of work. He had spent a long time preparing his remarks; but were they going to have the desired effect? Indeed, any effect at all?

"I'd like to thank the conference sponsors for asking me to speak this morning. They have asked me to talk about the experience of our little retirement home, in its first 18 months and whether I think our 'model' has much relevance for others. I will try to do that but briefly. I also want to offer some thoughts on 3 wider issues.

I apologise in advance if anyone is offended by my remarks. The industry had to cope with some appalling problems during the COVID-19 crisis; and many of you present have probably done more for what used to be called the public good in the last few months than you will ever do again. It is hard then to be criticised and actually my comments are aimed at systems, not individuals.

I am aware of that and also for the fact that a lot is going to be squeezed into the next 15 minutes. On this last point, I should note that I am paying for my words to be printed in tomorrow's paper, so you can reread my remarks there if you do find them too dense now. It will be the only time in my life that I have behaved like one of those Middle Eastern princes who pay newspapers to print their peons of self-praise to get magazine coverage. The difference is that, from me, there is very little praise of anyone or anything in what I am paying to have reproduced.

So, the first question for me to address is this. Is The Four Winds the shape for looking after the elderly in years to come? My answer to that is an unequivocal 'no'. I think The Four Winds will be thriving as much as any retirement village in 10 years' time; that's not the issue. COVID19 could have derailed us, as – before that – so could the unsought bid for Ingham's. But we escaped the bid and, during the crisis, we had help when we needed it on essentials like getting hold of PPE. I'd especially like to mention our old owner, WH, in that regard for the help they gave us. The overall lesson of these 18 months to me though is that, for a firm like Ingham's, it's possible to provide a viable retirement village for the families of long-time workers.

The problem, quite simply is that, in a business world of the kind we now have, of zero contracts and gig workers, there just are never going to be enough firms like Ingham's to finance and run more than a handful of such Villages. I very much hope that, in the coming years, things like zero hours will be outlawed, to restore a better relationship between employer and employee. But, even if that happens, I doubt we will ever – or should ever – go back to a world in which most workers stay with one firm long enough to make corporate retirement homes like The Four Winds a viable option. The Four Winds is a side turning in the evolutionary cycle of care for the elderly, not the way forward.

Indeed, I think we have to have a complete rethinking of the way in which care for the elderly is currently provided and how it is financed. The whole care market needs to shift, which will have enormous implications for all of you.

This is my second issue. It is a huge and emotive subject. It will pitch the old against the young and the elderly wealthy against the poor. A handful of politicians have flirted with ideas over the last few years for some kind of 'grand bargain', a new social contract. But even these tentative moves have collapsed as soon as the opposition of those who will be adversely affected begins to show itself. We are going to have to do much better than that in future. A new structure will have to command political support across the spectrum. It also has to assure younger people, who are bound to end up paying for much of it, that the same 'good deal' will be there for them when it's their turn. Otherwise, they have no incentive to take part. And, as if that wasn't enough, any new structure will have to convince the rich elderly that they should, indeed they must, pay for anything they want above the national minimum.

Given, at the moment, we can in this country barely be courteous to those who disagree with us, this is a huge ask all round. And it's only one 'ask' out of several. In my view, and this my third 'issue', there also has to be a complete revamp of the whole tax structure in the UK. Without that, we will not be able to deal with the flagrant social inequalities that the recent crisis has again so clearly thrown up. Add in the other challenges the country will have to face, such as the need to start to tackle the issue of climate change and the staggering innovations that are coming from Artificial Intelligence; and I have to say I'm actually quite glad that I am too old and ill to have to grapple with all of this.

I said at the beginning that I would only talk for 15 minutes. So let me end by reprising the 3 major issues that I think have to be dealt with just in the context of the industry we are today to talk about.

First, of course it makes sense to bring the elderly sick together, to provide good and cost-effective specialist care. But I have come to the conclusion that we've gone too far in air-brushing all the elderly (sick and well) out of the general picture and into specialised places. Life is meant to be lived among all sorts of people of all sorts of ages. I don't know if there is a single model that will do this better than now. But I certainly commend to your attention the experiment already going on in the Netherlands where students are living among the elderly, getting rent-free accommodation while at college, in return for time they spend with the elderly. What I think is inevitable is that – post COVID-19 – fit elderly people will no longer be prepared to shut themselves away, in places where a Government can effectively turn the key on them for a year or more and prevent the one thing that makes life worth living for most of them, close links with their family.

Second, the money side of care also has to be completely reviewed. Care has to be recognised and valued wherever it is given and whoever it is given by, whether or not money changes hands.

We will never get a system agreed across the generations unless and until a daughter's freely given help to an ailing mother is recognised and rewarded, just like the payment of a professional carer. We will never get a viable system until carers are adequately paid and protected. We will never get a system the country can afford unless there is an agreed national minimum of care financed from taxation, with all 'extras' being paid for by those who want it and are prepared to pay for it. To get the buy-in of the rich will, I think, in turn require a complete reform of the inheritance tax system, which makes life-long involvement in a State-run care system the key to (probably) the total elimination of all death duties of any kind. There needs to be a balance; unambiguous commitment to pay while people age but the prospect that, by doing this, they can pass their money on as they wish, when they die.

Finally, I am convinced that the State needs to completely revamp the tax structure on which this and many other industries now operate. I accept that the care sector needs corporate muscle to provide volume and resilience. 'Mom and Pop' operations in care homes will have their place as they do now. But corporates, most of whom will, understandably, be profit-seekers are needed too. What has to change is the whole basis of financing and taxing companies in industries like this. No more should we allow companies to run up vast levels of corporate debt, get tax relief on the interest and effectively force the public sector to pay for the debt interest because the weekly care charges have to cover the interest. Either that, or the whole shoddy edifice will come crashing down. Here, now, I will just identify 2 elements of what I think will be needed – for this area of business and across the whole corporate sector.

First, after a transition period to allow firms to adjust their balance sheets, especially to adjust their borrowing, disallow all interest payments in the calculation of corporate tax. Maybe one could combine that with the sweetener of a lower Corporation Tax rate, as companies migrate to the new system. And, second, Government must prohibit the use of tax evasion and avoidance through the use of tax havens. My guess is that, by size, half the industry here uses debt interest and tax havens, so I realise that what I am saying will be unwelcome to put it politely.

I have had my 15 minutes. As I said earlier, there is a huge amount to change and, as with how to integrate the elderly better into the community, it's not even clear sometimes what needs to be. What we mustn't do is go back to the old pre-COVID-19 days of working. Nor must we quail at the size of the task, just because it is huge. You will all have heard the story of the Treasury Minister who left a note for his successor, saying "Sorry, we've spent all the money". The note my generation needs to leave the next is rather different. It needs to say "Sorry. We had the best of motives but we screwed up. What we did is no longer fit for purpose." And it's in that spirit that I, for one, intend to quit the stage and leave this huge task to those younger and better able than I to start to tackle these problems.